J.T. SPANNER THOUGHT HE'D SEEN THE WORST NEW YORK HAD TO OFFER

"Suddenly headlights appeared out of nowhere shining blindingly through the rear window of the T-Bird.

Christ, please, not a cop car.

The car behind swerves out, streaks past in a blur of speed, doing at least 80 up the bridge incline ahead.

The stupid sonofabitch is going to crash, sure as hell.

The car ahead is at the top of the bridge, still in sight, when it swings sharply toward the railing on the near side. One of the car's rear doors flies open. A large object catapults out the door. The object—it's a body—arcs through the air toward the railing . . ."

VITAL STATISTICS

Thomas Chastain

CHARTER
NEW YORK

A DIVISION OF CHARTER COMMUNICATIONS INC.
A GROSSET & DUNLAP COMPANY

VITAL STATISTICS

Copyright © 1977 by Thomas Chastain
All rights reserved

Published by arrangement with Quadrangle/The
New York Times Book Co., Inc.

Charter Books
A Division of Charter Communications Inc.
A Grosset & Dunlap Company
360 Park Avenue South
New York, New York 10010

Manufactured in the United States of America

To
Leonard Franklin
My Friend
and
Wise Counselor

Mens cujusque is est quisque.
A man's mind is the man himself.
—Latin proverb

THE city is located at latitude 40°42′45″, longitude 74°0′23″, is 320 square miles in area, has a population of about 8,000,000, and temperatures from an average low of 33.2° to an average high of 76.8°.

With Manhattan as the hub, the spokes of the city fan out north, south, and east to the boroughs, The Bronx, Brooklyn, Staten Island, and Queens.

Of the city's population, 48 percent are either foreign-born or have one parent who was foreign-born, 14 percent of the population are black, 7.8 percent Puerto Rican.

The city is a triple-tiered structure: at ground level, there are 6,000 miles of streets, 578 miles of shoreline; below ground, 134 miles of subways, 10 miles of tunnels; above ground, 33 buildings which rise 50 or more floors in height, 65 bridges, ranging from 34 feet in length to over 4,000 feet in length.

The city is a presence . . .

> ... The Queensboro Bridge is a cantile-
> vered bridge, measures 1,182 feet in length,
> towers 135 feet above the river, was com-
> pleted in 1909, ranks eighth in size of New
> York's bridges, all eight of which are
> among the world's leading bridges ...

IT is a humid night, at 12:17 A.M.—early morning, actually—early in June, the sky overcast. Most of the streets in Queens are silent and deserted, the pavements slick with moisture from the mist lingering on the wind from the south which has brought earlier showers. The T-Bird's speedometer flickers between 55 and 60. Here and there on the streets rain puddles reflect a liquid image of light from the corner lampposts and the fuzzy glow of neon signs outside the few places still open—a bar and grill, a fast-food joint, an all-night supermarket, a Chinese restaurant, a massage parlor—as they flash by outside the car windows.

The approach to the Queensboro Bridge comes into view up ahead, the ornate gridwork of bridge lights strung out high across the dark flow of the East River. Beyond the bridge the skyline of Manhattan thrusts up a sawtoothed ridge of dazzling brightness out of the lowering mists.

As the T-Bird starts up the bridge, a bus passes going in the opposite direction, its whooshing sound trailing after like a mournful sigh as its taillights disappear down the bridge toward Queens. There are no other cars in sight ahead or behind.

Crossing the bridge, high above the river, in darkness, creates a sensation of being suspended in mid-air inside a giant steel cage; where there's no above or below, only a black void.

Suddenly, a pair of headlights appears out of nowhere shining blindingly in through the rear window of the T-Bird.

Christ, please, not a cop car.

The car behind swerves out, streaks past in a blur of speed, rear end sluing almost out of control, doing at least 80 up the bridge incline ahead.

The stupid sonofabitch is going to crash, sure as hell.

The car ahead is at the top of the bridge, still in sight, when it swings sharply toward the railing on the near side. One of the car's rear doors flies open. A large object catapults out the door. The object—it's a body—arcs through the air toward the railing. It almost clears the top of the railing, with the river down below on the far side, and then the torso slams against one of the bridge stanchions and the body falls, sprawled, back onto the bridge.

The speeding car is well past where the body was tossed out. It slows for a moment; then, with a jerking motion, careens away over the bridge toward Manhattan.

It's useless to try to chase the car. And maybe the victim's still alive and can be helped.

The headlights of the T-Bird are focused on the body, a couple of feet away. The body—stripped bare—is that of a female with dark hair.

Out on the bridge, looking at her up close, she—whoever she was—is now little more than a hunk of raw meat. She's lying askew on her back. Her legs are outspread. The left arm is flung back above the head, the hand open, palm-upward. The right arm is twisted out of sight under the body. Most of the torso is splattered with blood, and where it isn't, the flesh is scored by small puckered holes. The palm of the open hand is disfigured by the same small puckered holes. There's a faint stink of scorched flesh emanating from the body. The forehead is unscarred, but beneath it—where the face should have been—is only a jellied mass of crimson dermis.

The pain she had to have suffered in her dying is almost palpable in the dark air; the echo of her last, anguished screams of terror sound and resound in the mind.

A car passes, slowing as it comes by and then speeding away.

Another car coming over the bridge from Queens has pulled up and parked behind the T-Bird. A man gets out of the car and comes along the bridge and around in front of the T-Bird. He's a big, muscular man, not older than fifty, gray-haired, wearing slacks, sneakers, and a denim windbreaker. He zips up the windbreaker as he approaches, saying, "You got car trouble? Need any help?"

"I—ah—thanks. My car's all right. The trouble is this."

The man sees the body for the first time. He takes a couple of confused steps backward, retches, and for a moment looks like he's going to be sick. He gulps down air, wipes a sleeve across his mouth, an expression of fear on his face.

"It's all right, friend. I had nothing to do with what's happened here. The body was tossed out of a car crossing the bridge ahead of me. I think whoever was in the car meant to dump the body in the river. They missed and the car sped away. Did you happen to spot a car back there, traveling fast, when you were headed for the bridge?"

The man shakes his head. He's still half-sick and scared.

"Look, pal, take it easy. I'm going to call the police now. I'm a private investigator myself. I've got a phone in my car. Hang around, will you, huh?"

He doesn't say anything, but he nods his head.

He's pacing back and forth in front of the T-Bird, glancing in through the windshield nervously from time to time when the call on the car phone to the 911 police emergency number goes through and a voice answers:

"Police operator."

"Yeah, I want to report a body lying on the lower level of the Queensboro Bridge. In the middle of the bridge. Dead. The body was dumped out of a speeding car. I happened to see it happen."

"Queensboro Bridge? Dead body?"

"Right. My name's J. T. Spanner. I'm a licensed private investigator. I'll be here when the cars come."

"They're on their way," the police operator says and hangs up.

There's the sound of a motor starting up behind the T-Bird, and the guy in the windbreaker speeds past in his car without a sideward glance and is quickly out of sight across the bridge. He's obeying the old protect-your-own-ass axiom: don't get involved.

Fuck you, too, *friend*.

A couple of more cars pass by and speed on without slowing down. Somewhere upriver a foghorn croaks. Far in the distance, there's a wail of sirens. The exposed body, mist settling on it, looks cold and forlorn lying on the wet steel girders. More sirens sound in the night; some a long way away, others nearer.

Two squad cars are the first to arrive, sweeping in from Manhattan up over the crest of the bridge, red dome lights rotating as they cut across from south lane to north lane and skid to a stop, headlights facing the T-Bird's headlights, with the body lying between.

The four uniformed patrolmen come over, looking down at the body, looking up, nodding, looking around at the bridge, one of them asking, "You the party who called in about the body?"

"Yeah. Spanner's the name."

"Uh-huh," he says. "Homicide's on the way. They'll have some questions for you."

The patrolman who's spoken goes back to his squad car and gets on the radio. The other three walk in slow circles around the body, as if they hoped to discover something new by viewing it from different angles.

More cars arrive, sirens screaming, a couple of unmarked Ford Fairlanes, a paneled police van, four more squad cars. There are almost two dozen policemen milling around the body on the bridge; half of them uniformed, half in plainclothes. One of the men from the forensic unit is fiddling with a camera, preparing to take pictures. A plainclothesman dressed in a gray Dacron suit with a lieutenant's badge clipped to his lapel strides over.

"You the fellow who called in about the body?" he asks.

"Yeah. I'm J. T. Spanner. I'm a private investigator. Here's my license. I saw the body get tossed out of a car."

He takes a careful look at the license, nods, and introduces himself. "Lieutenant Cortez, Sixteenth Precinct Homicide."

Cortez is about six feet tall, weighs around 190, has black hair, clipped short, and a complexion the color of mahogany. He's chewing on an unlit inch-long cigar butt.

His attention is momentarily distracted when another squad car pulls up and a tall man in plainclothes gets out of the back seat of the car. Some of the policemen ringing the body step back out of the way to let the tall man through. He settles on his haunches beside the body. One of the assistant medical examiners, probably.

Cortez looks back and takes out a notebook and a pen. "Okay, Spanner, why don't you tell me what you saw?"

"I was driving in through Queens. Less than—oh, say twenty minutes ago. Just as I reached the approach to the bridge back there, this car zooms up right on my tail, swings around me, and must have been doing about eighty across the bridge ahead of me. When the car reached the spot where the body is now—I still had it in clear sight—one of the car doors—the rear door on the passenger side—swings open, and this body comes hurtling out. The body almost went over the railing into the river, but it hit on that brace there and fell back onto the bridge. The car hightailed it out of here. I don't think I could have caught it, but anyway I stopped to investigate the body. It was just like you see it there. I called in from the phone in my car."

"You didn't touch the body?"

"I know better than that."

"There were no other cars, witnesses, around at the time, huh?" Cortez asks.

"Not then, no. A couple passed after I had stopped, but they kept going. One guy did stop, but then, while I was calling the police, he must have panicked. He drove away fast."

"About this car the body was thrown from—did you get a good look at it, at anybody inside?"

"It all happened in a hell of a flash, lieutenant. It was a big car, dark color, a Buick, maybe, would be my impression. I'd guess there were two or more people inside—again an impression. There wasn't much time and a lot was happening. From the time it passed me, I was never close enough to get a good look, and then it was gone."

Cortez grunts. "You said the body almost went over the railing there before it hit the brace and fell on the bridge. You sure about that?"

"I'm sure. From what I saw, there is no doubt that whoever dumped the body meant for it to go into the river. It was just sheerest luck it didn't."

"Anything else?"

"That's about all I can think of."

Cortez scratches his cheek with the cap of his pen. "Uh—you want to give me a brief account of your movements this evening?"

"Yeah. I've been out on the Island for the past couple of days with three other guys. I own a fourth of a house and a fourth of a boat out there. The fishing was good until the rain started this afternoon. I left there about six-thirty P.M. One of the guys drove in with me. I dropped him in Garden City, where he lives. John Macauley. He's a lawyer—Hogarth, Whittaker, Macauley. Sometimes I do investigative work for the firm. The office is on Madison Avenue. After I dropped Macauley off, I drove straight on in to here. Macauley lives at Seven-Nine-Three Cedar Lane, Garden City. You can check him there or at his office tomorrow."

"And *your* office is where?"

"The Graybar Building, Lexington Avenue. Room Thirteen-Thirteen."

"Okay." Cortez closes the notebook and shoves it and the pen into his coat pocket. "Stick around for a minute, okay?"

He goes back over and stands talking to the man who's probably the assistant medical examiner. Most of the policemen who have been gathered around the body have moved back a few paces. The photographer, camera aimed at the corpse, is popping flashbulbs.

Now that the police and squad cars are at the scene, every car that's come over the bridge within the last few minutes has stopped, and some of the drivers and passengers have gotten out to gawk. Several of the uniformed patrolmen are trying to get the people back into their cars and to clear the bridge.

Another paneled van, dark gray in color, appears in view from the direction of Manhattan. It makes a semi-U-turn in the middle of the bridge and backs up close to the body. On the side of the van are printed the words:

NEW YORK CITY
DEPT. OF HOSPITALS
MORTUARY DIVISION

The driver and his assistant get out and swing open the van's rear-receiving doors.

Lieutenant Cortez returns. His face is grim. He says, "Jesus, somebody sure dumped on her, from what the assistant M.E. says. She was beaten to death, all right, according to his preliminary opinion. Along with some other stuff."

"You mean like those small holes on her body? I was curious about them."

"Burn marks. He says it looks like somebody must have tortured her repeatedly with the lit end of a cigarette. Even on the palms of her hands and the soles of her feet. Most of her teeth have been knocked out, too. He found four or five of them lodged in her throat."

He pauses and then says, "I guess you can leave now. If we have any other questions, we'll contact you."

He turns away. The guys on the morgue wagon are loading the body into the back of the van.

R.I.P.—faceless lady—you've earned it.

> Weather: Hot, humid today, thundershowers in the late afternoon, rain tonight. Clear and hot tomorrow. Temperature range: today 70–90 . . .
>
> ——*Late City Edition*, The New York Times

SITTING at her desk in the outer office, Ellie looks up, smiles happily, and says, "Welcome back, J. T."

She gets up from the desk, comes over and offers her lips for a kiss.

Dressed for the hot weather, as she is this day, Ellie looks more like nineteen than twenty-nine, her actual age. She's wearing a pale turquoise shirtdress gathered at the waist by an obi sash. The sash pulls the blouse of the dress snugly over her firm, full breasts and the skirt stops at her knees. She's bare-legged and wears flat sandals. Her toenails are tinted the same blush-pink color as her fingernails and lipstick. She has her dark hair pulled back from her forehead in a ponytail which gives her face an open, young-girl prettiness. The only jewelry she has on is a wedding band on the third finger of her left hand which she still wears although she's the first ex-Mrs. J. T. Spanner.

Drawing her head back, she asks, "How was the fishing?"

"Oh, you know how the line goes: we got a lot of bites. Mosquito bites, chigger bites . . . No, seriously, it was a good couple of days."

"You kind of extended it for another half-day of sleep, huh?" She glances up at the wall clock. The time is 11:45 A.M. "Didn't you get any rest while you were gone?"

"Oh, I got plenty of rest while I was there. The problem was after I got back last night. The goddamnedest thing happened. When I was coming in over the Queensboro Bridge, somebody in a car ahead of me tried to dump a body in the river. Except the body didn't go into the river; it landed on the bridge. It was a woman's body. She'd been beaten and pretty well disfigured. The car got away."

"You're kidding!"

"No. The truth. I got hung up for a long time afterward with the police. Then when I got home I couldn't sleep, even after several stiff slugs of Jack Daniel's. Couldn't get the image of that body out of my mind."

"How horrible." Ellie shakes her head. "Do they know who she was?"

"They didn't when I left there. In addition to everything else, the body was nude, nothing at the scene to identify her. And her face was a mess—hardly recognizable as human. The afternoon papers'll probably have something on it."

"Horrible," Ellie says again.

"Yeah, well, it's a police problem now. Speaking of problems, anything been going on around here since I spoke to you yesterday? Any new business coming up?"

Ellie trails along into the inner office. "No problems. You did get one phone call this morning, though. About a half hour ago. A Mrs. Margaret Balfe. B–A–L–F–E. She said she wanted to talk to you. She left a phone number."

"Balfe? I don't know the name. You can get her for me, though."

"Oh," Ellie says, "and the check from Macauley's office for the Charnnord case still didn't come in this morning."

"Well, give them a call. They've got plenty of money over there."

Ellie nods. "I'll get the call to that Mrs. Balfe for you now." She goes back to the outer office.

She's hardly closed the door before the intercom on the desk buzzes and she says, "I have a call for you from a Lieutenant Cortez at the Sixteenth Precinct."

"All right, honey. Put him through."

"I'll hold on the other call until you're finished."

Cortez's voice on the phone says, "Mr. Spanner?"

"Yeah, what can I do for you, lieutenant?"

"About that body last night—there've been a couple of new developments in the case since." He pauses for a moment and then says, "I want to ask you: that car you spotted the body coming out of. Could it have been a Toyota—a Toyota Corolla?"

"No. No way. It was a much larger car than that. I would have recognized a Toyota, or at least that it was a small car, even fast as things happened."

"You're sure of that?" There's a note of disappointment in his voice. "Absolutely sure?"

"Yeah. Positive. What makes it important that it wasn't a Toyota?"

There's another pause on the line before Cortez says slowly, "A kinky thing happened while the morgue wagon was on its way to the M.E.'s office at Bellevue with the body. Right at the foot of the Queensboro Bridge, on Second Avenue, this Toyota Corolla pulls up alongside the morgue wagon. Two characters are in the car, waving guns. The characters are wearing stocking masks and khaki coveralls. They force the morgue wagon driver to pull around on Fifty-ninth Street under the bridge. Then one of the perpetrators holds the driver and his assistant at gunpoint while the other one removes the body from the morgue wagon and puts it in the car. The perpetrators took the keys to the morgue wagon before speeding away. You ever hear anything like it?"

"Jesus, no. And nobody else saw any of this going on?"

"There weren't that many people around last night at that hour," Cortez says. "The morgue guys think the Toyota followed them over the bridge, or must have been waiting for them. I thought maybe if you thought the car you saw was a Toyota, it could have been the same car."

"No, it couldn't have been a Toyota I saw. But I still don't understand. Why the hell would anybody want to steal the body from the morgue wagon?"

"The best we can come up with is that either somebody didn't want the corpse identified, or that they were afraid some incriminating evidence had been left on the body when it didn't go into the river."

"I don't know, lieutenant."

"I don't know, either," Cortez says. "Another thing that's happened meantime is that in the early hours of the morning some woman reported to the Bronx precinct her daughter disappeared. The daughter was a stewardess. She got into JFK Airport at nine P.M. last night and seems to have vanished. Because it was JFK, in Queens, and the body turned up on the Queensboro Bridge, we brought the mother to this precinct this morning and showed her the pictures we shot of the body last night. The mother said that from looking at the pictures we had, it wasn't her daughter. But how the hell could anybody make an I.D. from the photos the shape that body was in? Probably just a coincidence, anyway."

"Yeah. But how about a comparison of fingerprints? There must be existing fingerprints on the stewardess."

There's a long silence on the line. Cortez coughs before he says, "Forensic doesn't always make prints of the victim on the scene. Sometimes they wait till the body's at the morgue. That's what happened last night—only, of course, they didn't know the body was never going to reach the morgue. How the hell could they?"

"That's one hell of a police department you guys are running there—I'll say that for you."

"When one thing fucks up, everything fucks up," Cortez says patiently. "You know that; you were a cop yourself once. Which reminds me; how come last night you didn't mention you were once on the force and worked out of the one-six?"

"It didn't seem pertinent. You didn't know me back then; I didn't know you."

"Well, anyhow, if you think of anything else about last night, or the car, we'd like to hear. Oh, and listen—Captain John Tynan, head of Homicide here, will be handling the case from now on. He's got a copy of your statement. He may want to talk to you later."

"Yeah, okay."

Cortez hangs up.

What a bunch of Keystone Kops. First, they've got the body, then they lose it. They don't take prints, they can't make an ID, all they've got is a bunch of photos, Jesus—

The intercom buzzes again. "I have Mrs. Balfe on the line," Ellie says.

"Who?"

"Mrs. Balfe. You know the woman—"

"Oh, yeah. Fine. I'll talk to her."

On the phone, voice shaky, a woman says, "Hello, Mr. Spanner?"

"Yes, this is J. T. Spanner. You called me earlier, Mrs. Balfe?"

"You *are* the private detective who discovered that girl's body on the bridge last night, this morning?" she asks. "The police told me. Is that correct?"

"The police told you? Well, yes, that's correct. May I ask what is your interest?"

"My daughter disappeared last night. At John F. Kennedy Airport. I reported her disappearance to the police.

They had me down to the precinct this morning and showed me photographs of a body and said you were the one who called them about it—"

"Oh, yes, your daughter is an airline stewardess. Now I understand. I was just talking to Lieutenant Cortez at the Sixteenth Precinct. He told me about you, about your daughter. What is it you wanted to know from me?"

Her voice is firmer. "I want to hire you. To look for my daughter. I'd like to see you, to talk to you. I live in the North Bronx."

"Uh—look, Mrs. Balfe, if she disappeared only last night, she hasn't been missing all that long, you know."

"If you knew my daughter, Mr. Spanner, you'd understand my concern. Jill *always* calls me the minute she gets in from a flight. *Always*. She—Jill—lives in an apartment in Manhattan with two other girls—stewardesses—and they haven't heard from her, either. They're upset about her disappearance, too, and so are the police, I think, now that I've talked to them."

There's a pause on the line, the sound of a deep, indrawn breath, and she goes on. "That wasn't Jill's body—the pictures they showed me—but I am worried that *something* has happened to her. When the police mentioned your name, that you were a private detective, I decided to call you. I just *have* to know what's happened to Jill. Won't you please help me?"

"Well, I *am* interested, Mrs. Balfe—"

"I know you expect to be paid," she says quickly. "I'll pay you whatever your fee is—"

"I charge one hundred and fifty dollars a day."

"That's quite satisfactory. You will come see me now?"

"Yes. I can be up there within the next couple of hours. What's the address?"

"I live at Nine Hundred Thirteen West Two-hundred-fifty-ninth Street. That's the block just west of Arlington Avenue, the North Bronx."

"I have it, Mrs. Balfe. I know the general area. I'll see you shortly."

"Thank you, Mr. Spanner."

As soon as Mrs. Balfe hangs up, the office door opens and Ellie comes in.

"What were those calls about?" she asks.

"You won't believe it, kid. The call from Lieutenant Cortez was to let me know the latest developments on that body I told you about. It seems that while the morgue wagon was enroute from the bridge to the medical examiner's office with the body, somebody hijacked it—snatched the body."

"You mean they stole the dead body?"

"Uh-huh. Then Cortez told me that early this morning some woman reported her daughter was missing since last night. The daughter was a stewardess; she disappeared from JFK Airport last night. You'll read all the facts when you type up the notes I made of the conversation. But that ain't all, honey—"

"So, tell me, tell me."

"That Mrs. Balfe. *She's* the mother of the missing airline stewardess. She got my name from the police. She says, after looking at the police photographs of the body from the bridge, that it isn't her daughter. But she wanted to hire me to look for her daughter. You'll read all that in the notes, too."

Ellie's eyes are shining with excitement. "Of course you accepted her case."

"What you do mean 'of course'? I almost didn't. A missing persons—chances are it's strictly routine, probably won't amount to a damn."

"You can't kid me, J. T. I know when something has a hold on you, like that body on the bridge does. Getting hired to look for this missing girl gives you a legitimate opportunity to involve yourself in the case. Even with the cops."

"Go on, get out of here. I have to get ready to *schlepp* up to the Bronx to see Mrs. Balfe."

Ellie takes the piece of paper covered with the scrawled notes of the two telephone conversations. She frowns. "That means you won't be able to have lunch with Lee and me, I guess. Huh?"

"Oh, Christ, honey, I'm sorry. I forgot. Listen, you and Lee go ahead and have lunch. Explain to Lee, will you? And take the money out of petty cash."

Ellie nods and goes back to the outer office.

Lee is the second ex-Mrs. J. T. Spanner. There are only two of them—Eleanor Stanton Spanner and Lee Coates Spanner—and, thank God, there are no laws against bigamous divorces. Between them, Ellie and Lee run the office of *J. T. Spanner Private Investigations* (you could say they each have a stake in the business since they both collect alimony), and the two of them are best friends. A smart-ass acquaintance once summed up the arrangement by saying: "J. T., you're the only character I ever heard of divorced two wives and the three of you lived happily *ménage à trois* ever after."

In the office, with the windows up—and Ellie hadn't turned on the air conditioner—it feels like the weatherman's going to luck out on his forecast. In the stagnant air, the drapes hang like a still life framed by the open windows while dust and heat and traffic noises from Lexington Avenue thirteen floors below seep into the room. At an angle across the street the sun strikes shafts of refracted light from the windowpanes of the Chrysler Building. A couple of pigeons flutter lazily out of the sky, waddle along the ledge outside the office long enough to shake the dust from their feathers into the open windows, then flap off into the sun.

". . . Hello? J. T.?" Ellie's standing in the open doorway. "I spoke to you three times and you didn't hear me."

"Sorry, honey, I was daydreaming. Maybe you should

have said 'Ahoy, there.' Did you know that when Alexander Graham Bell first invented the telephone he thought people should answer by saying, 'Ahoy, there!'? That's true."

"Your mind is sure crammed with a lot of curious information, J. T." She shakes her head. "Listen, I just read over your notes. I want you to find out who did all those awful things to that poor girl—and why."

"Hey, hold on, honey! All I'm being hired for is to look for a missing female. There may be no connection between the two cases."

"I'll bet you a month's alimony it's the same person," Ellie says firmly. Then she says, "And that reminds me: I'll have to put lunch on my credit card, and you can settle up with me later. There's not enough in petty cash to pay for lunch for Lee and me."

"Baby, baby. You really know how to stick it to a guy, don't you?"

Ellie pushes the door wide, a mischievous smile on her face. "If I do," she says teasingly, "it's only in return for the other night at my place. Remember?" She does a bump with her pelvis. "Like tit"—turns and does a grind with her bottom—"for tat."

Still smiling, as she goes back out the door, she looks over her shoulder and adds, "Why, J. T., I do believe you're actually blushing." Her laughter carries through the closed door.

Women. But then, like the man said, you can't live with them and you can't live without them. Or was it a woman who said that? Probably.

> ... In New York City, including the 5 boroughs of Manhattan, Brooklyn, The Bronx, Queens, and Staten Island, the annual rate of homicide is about 21 per 100,000 of population, an average of four-plus persons murdered each day ...

THE house where Margaret Balfe lives on West 259th Street is one of a block-long row of well-preserved buildings, all of them three and four stories high, of yellow-face brick, and of another era—of the era when fancy ornamented facades and windows of stained glass were all the vogue of Upper Bronx upper-middle-class houses in the early 1900s. There is, fortunately, a parking space for the T-Bird directly across the street from Number 913.

It has been comfortable enough in the car on the drive uptown with the air conditioner turned on high but now, out on the street, the summer day is full of prickly heat and sun glare. The sidewalks are deserted, and it's quiet for the length of the block.

The Balfe house has three stone steps bracketed by wrought-iron handrails leading up to a low stone stoop. The front door is of dark metal, polished and shined so it gleams with the wet-look of black vinyl, and to the right of the door is a bell. The bell makes a muted, musical sound somewhere in the interior of the house like the tinkling of wind chimes.

The woman who answers the bell opens the door on a chain and asks, "Yes?"

"Mrs. Balfe? I'm J. T. Spanner—"

"Oh, yes, I was expecting you." She unchains and opens the door. "Please come in."

There is a second woman, wizened and white-haired, standing behind her. The old woman moves to one side while Margaret Balfe closes and chains the door again, then leads the way down a long hall to a spacious sitting room in the back of the house. The white-haired woman, frail and wrinkled and stooped under layers of years, brings up the rear. Here where the windows face south, the shades are drawn against the sun, and the subdued light makes the room seem cooler than it is.

Margaret Balfe fans the air with her hand. "Isn't the heat awful? This is about the only room in the house you can breathe in. I hope you're not too uncomfortable."

"No, it's fine here."

Margaret Balfe is about 5'5" tall, probably in her late fifties, and too fat by fifty pounds. She's wearing a flowing, ankle-length caftan of cotton, with red, green, and white stripes. Her hair is black—an obviously dyed black-black. She has it pinned up on the top of her head except for a few straggly strands and there are glistening beads of perspiration along the hairline. Her eyes are two blue marbles embedded in the pudgy, pale flesh of her face. Take away the fat and her face might be passably attractive. She appears stolid, but there's a suggestion of inner anxiety in the meaningless smile which flickers on and off her lips like a nervous tic.

She fiddles with the collar of her caftan, lifting it from the back of her damp neck, and says, "I guess you know I appreciate your coming to see me. I've been almost out of my mind with worry most of the night and today. I'm a widow, and Jill and I have always been so close. My husband's been dead for ten years now."

She looks as if she's going to weep. She shakes her head. She notices the old woman standing behind her and pulls her forward. "This is my mother-in-law, Mrs. Edward Balfe, Senior. She lives here with me." In a loud voice directed at her mother-in-law, Margaret Balfe says, "This—is—Mr.—Spanner—Mother—Balfe—I—told—you—about—him—and—Jill—our—Jill."

The old woman bobs her head and offers a palsied hand that is like brittle, aged parchment to the touch. She is wearing a long black crepe-de-chine dress. Her snow-white hair, twisted into a tight knot at the back of her head, has thinned so much that there's more scalp than hair showing on her skull. Her eyes staring myopically out of the age-ravaged face appear milky-colored.

"You'll bring my granddaughter home, yes?" she asks, head bobbing.

"I'm—going—to—try—to—bring—Jill—home—yes."

The head bobs again.

"She doesn't really understand all this," Margaret Balfe says. She takes the old woman by the arm. "Come—on—Mother—Balfe—you—rest—now—while—Mr.—Spanner—and—I—have—a—nice—talk." She steers her mother-in-law toward the door to the hall, saying: "I'll be right back, Mr. Spanner. Please make yourself at home."

The room looks like a solarium in a home for the aged. The furniture—the upholstered armchairs, wooden rockers, two sofas; one leather, the other covered in velvet corduroy—is mismatched and slightly shabby. Two color television sets stand against the far wall of the room, both sets switched on, to different channels, with the sound turned down. Near the windows is a collection of dusty potted plants, all of them in need of pruning, and none of them too healthy-looking. The windows are floor-to-ceiling. There are six windows and they're hung with what were once white—and are now drab gray—batiste curtains. Opposite the windows, on the back wall, hangs a painting of the Virgin Mary. Just beneath the painting is a small rectory table, and on the table is a votive candle and a string of rosary beads. In the heat of the day the room is filled with a pervasive odor of candle drippings, floor wax, mildew, and what was probably an earlier spraying of air freshener.

Separating the two television sets, in the center of the room, is a large fireplace with a marble mantel. On the mantel is a group of framed photographs. One of the photographs is a wedding picture; the bride in a lacy white gown, the groom in a morning coat. The bride is Margaret Balfe: younger, slimmer, a happy expectant smile on her face which is, sure enough, a quite attractive face. The groom is unsmiling, his hair is black with long sideburns, his jaw square, and his eyes dark and serious-looking. He is about an inch shorter than she.

The rest of the photographs are of the same girl—almost certainly Jill Balfe—at various stages of her life: nearly bald and barefooted in a frilly baby dress; at somewhere around age five or six in a bathing suit, top-heavy with baby fat, with the ocean in the background; shy and dimpled in a white confirmation dress; a few years older, on a pony, her smile showing braces on her teeth; in her teens, peering through an upraised tennis racquet; in her late teens, in jodhpurs on horseback, the baby fat and braces gone; later still, in a black graduation gown and mortarboard cap, face solemn; and, a last photograph, in color, in a stewardess's uniform and cap.

In the last photograph, the grown-up Jill Balfe makes a pretty picture. Her uniform—a gunmetal-gray gabardine—is stylishly cut, showing a lot of leg, and is molded to her 36–26–36 figure like a smooth coating of body paint. Her stewardess's cap is set at a jaunty angle atop her head. Beneath the cap, her hair is jet-black and she wears it short and curled under at the ends. Her eyes are amber. There's a certain slackness to the lower part of her face, giving her mouth a look as though it could sulk easily—a little more of the squareness of her father's jaw would have helped—still, she has enough going for her, face and body together, to never have to sleep alone except by choice.

Margaret Balfe has come silently back into the room and she says: "She is lovely, isn't she, my Jill?"

"Uh—yeah. Yes, she is. Very."

Margaret Balfe eases herself down on the leather sofa with the care of a woman closely attuned to the arbitrariness of her body and points to the armchair nearest her. "Have a seat, Mr. Spanner."

She's holding a manila envelope in her hand. She takes out a photograph of Jill Balfe in her stewardess's uniform—a copy of the photograph on the mantel—and passes it over. "I thought you might want this. It's her most recent picture. It was taken about a month ago."

"You said Jill lived in Manhattan, Mrs. Balfe. When was the last time you actually saw her?"

"That would be last Sunday. She came home here; we went to church together; she spent the day. The next day she had an assignment to fly overseas to Antwerp, Belgium. She got back from that flight last night."

"And when did you first discover she was missing?"

Margaret Balfe edges forward on the sofa. "Jill has always been punctual about calling me the minute she gets in from a flight. From the airport. She knows I worry. I knew she was due in about nine P.M. When I hadn't heard from her by eleven, I began to call and try to find out what had happened."

She pauses and shakes her head. "First, I called the airport. I found out the flight was in and that she'd been on it. I had her paged at the airport, and when she didn't answer, I began to call her apartment. I had to keep calling until eleven forty-five before I reached one of the girls who lives with her. She hadn't heard from Jill, either, and didn't know where she was."

She has trouble continuing and has to blink back the tears. "It—it—I was on the phone almost all last night. As it got later and later and there was still no word of Jill, both of her roommates also became alarmed. Both of them work for the same airline as Jill—U. S.-Global—and finally they were able to check and find out that she had gone through customs after the flight but that she had never checked in at the U.S.-G Airlines office at the airport as she was supposed to do." She makes a gesture of helplessness with her hand. "At three A.M. this morning I called the police and reported her missing."

"And what did the police tell you?"

Margaret Balfe plucks nervously at the collar of her caftan. "They didn't seem to take it very seriously. The officer I talked to tried to calm me down, said she'd probably call or turn up sooner or later, and that I should go to bed and try to get some sleep. Of course, I didn't. And then the police themselves at the Sixteenth Precinct called back about five A.M. and this time I could tell they *were* taking it seriously. They asked if I had a recent photograph of Jill and if they could send an officer to pick it up. Less than an hour later he came and got the photograph."

"Did the officer say anything at all to you about Jill, or why they wanted the photograph?"

"No, not then. It wasn't until about eight in the morning that they called again and asked if they could send a car to take me to the precinct house, that they wanted to talk to me about Jill. When I got there, it was the first time I heard about this body they'd found. They told me about how this body had been stolen. They wanted me to look at the photographs they'd taken of it, to see if I thought it could be Jill." She closes her eyes as if to block off the memory. *"Thank God it wasn't her!"* She's trembling now. She takes a deep breath to steady herself.

"Mrs. Balfe, I'm sorry to make you go through all this again. But I have to ask you: are you positive that the dead girl couldn't have been Jill?"

"Positive! Absolutely positive!" And there's such a note of finality in her voice that it's impossible to tell whether she's that certain of her identification of the body in the police photographs or whether she's permanently closed her mind to even the possibility that the dead girl could be her daughter.

"It wasn't Jill," she repeats emphatically.

"All right. Now, since then, who have you been in touch with at the police department?"

"There are two officers," she says. "Both at the Sixteenth Precinct in Manhattan. You know where it is? One is a Sergeant Hornstein—Murray Hornstein—in Missing Persons. I've been on the phone with him several times today. The other officer is in Homicide, in charge of the case of the body of the girl they found and lost, a Captain John Tynan. I've talked to him only once or twice—when he called to ask me some questions about Jill's friends, about her past life."

She has to pause again to catch her breath. "This heat," she says.

"Now, can you tell *me* about Jill? Where she was living in Manhattan, the names of the girls she was living with."

"She's still living, Mr. Spanner," Margaret Balfe corrects gently. "I believe that. She lives at 600 East 38th Street in Manhattan. Apartment 4J. It's what they call one of those luxury buildings. The three of them have a real nice place."

Her eyes wander around the sitting room briefly as if contrasting it with the luxury building on East 38th Street. Almost absently, she says, "Jill is always after me to move out of this old house. It's true I haven't kept it up very well. I would like to move, too, but what can I do as long as I have my mother-in-law?"

There's no answer to that, and she doesn't really expect one.

"Where was I?" she asks and then says, "Oh, yes, the

apartment. The other two girls who live with Jill are Karen Rushler and Barbara—they call her Bobbie—Gillian."

"How do you spell Gillian?"

"G–I–L–L–I–A–N."

"What about boyfriends? A boyfriend?"

She hesitates. "Well—she dates. She's always been popular. But I don't think there's any one special person. Or at least she hasn't said so. Whenever she mentions going here or there, it's always on a double date with one of her roommates."

"How about earlier boyfriends, other friends, when she still lived at home?"

"No, she never sees any of them, none of her old friends from the Bronx."

She's silent for a moment as if the thought troubles her. Then she says slowly, "At first, when she moved away from home it worried me. Still does, if the truth be known. She didn't tell me anything of her plans to become a stewardess until it had already happened. I tried to talk her out of it even then. But her mind was made up and I couldn't change it."

"Why were you opposed to her working as a stewardess, Mrs. Balfe?"

"Why?" She runs the palm of her right hand up the back of her neck under the overhang of pinned-up hair. "Well, I guess it was because—you know, the kind of life they lead. The odd hours they keep, the foreign places they fly to, all the different kinds of people they meet and deal with. I know I'm probably old-fashioned in some of my thinking, but it seems to me it increases the temptations."

She shakes her head slowly. "I'd always imagined Jill would make a good marriage while she was young. A doctor's wife, maybe. But then, things are so different in the world than since I was young. I guess I just have to face the fact that Jill's twenty-six years old now and a grown woman. Besides, I've always believed her to be a sensible person. She was raised in the church, and she had a strict upbringing. My husband and I saw to that. Of course, he spoiled her when he was alive. She was just the apple of his eye. Still, she never gave us a moment's trouble, all her life."

Her eyes are brimming with tears now, and her caftan is soaked through with perspiration.

"Just a couple of more questions now, Mrs. Balfe. The last time you saw Jill—did she seem all right, nothing troubling her?"

"Oh, she was fine, happy, laughing a lot. Just as she always is."

"I know you've had some time to think about it—do you know of any possible reason why she'd want to disappear voluntarily?"

"No. No, there just can't be."

"Is there anything else at all you want to tell me?"

"No. Truly."

"Well, we'll see what we can do. I don't know that I can be too optimistic. But I'll try. I'll take the photograph with me. If I have any news, I'll call you. If you need me, call my office. If you can't reach me and it's an emergency, I have a phone in my car. This card with my office address and phone number also has the car phone call letters on it. Just dial the operator and give her the information."

She nods and puts the card into a pocket of her caftan. She starts to struggle up from the sofa, and suddenly there's the sound of a high-pitched shriek from somewhere in the house, the anguished scream of a young girl. At first the words are unintelligible, and then they come clear in a shrill, piercing cry: "Listen! Listen! Listen to me! Why won't anybody listen to me?"

"My God! What's *that?*"

Margaret Balfe doesn't pause to answer. She's up on

her feet and moving along the hall so fast it's hard to keep up with her.

She hurries to the front hallway of the house and stops where there are two sliding doors on one side of the hall. She shoves the doors open and steps inside. In the gap between the doors, there's a space to see into the room. The shrill girlish screaming is coming from inside the room. The light is dim in there. All the shades are drawn at the windows, and the room is full of shadows except for the light from a small table lamp. The lamp illuminates the interior just enough to show the empty bookcases lining the four walls of what once must have been a small library and is now—furnished with a bed, a bureau, a couple of chairs and table—a bedroom. There's a sour odor emanating from the room, as of dried sweat, dust, and unwashed bedclothing.

The old woman—Mrs. Edward Balfe, Senior—is sitting on the side of the bed. She has her arms crossed over her chest, her body is rigid, and her eyes are staring sightlessly into space. Her lips appear not to move at all, but the voice coming from her throat is the voice of a very young girl speaking in a pronounced Irish brogue: "Jill wants to come home. Jill is lost. It's dark where she is, and she's scared. *Why won't anybody listen to me!*"

Jesus, it's eerie. That girlish, pubescent voice coming from the ancient, catatonic face.

Margaret Balfe leans over the old woman and says in a loud voice: "We—hear—you—Ardell—we—hear—you—Tell—Jill—we'll—find—her—Tell—Jill—Ardell."

"Now, did you hear that, Nora?" the girlish voice speaking from the old woman's mouth asks. "Ah, isn't that nice, Nora? Ah, now, isn't that nice?"

The old woman nods her head, her arms drop, her body slumps. Her eyes blink rapidly a couple of times, and she lies down on the bed and turns her head to the wall.

Margaret Balfe comes back to the door. She steps close.

"She'll be all right now," she says in a whisper. "She was in a trance. Mother Balfe has always been psychic. She was born with a caul over her eyes and has second sight. That was Ardell speaking through her. Ardell and Nora—that's Mother Balfe's given name—were twins. Ardell died of scarlet fever when she was thirteen. Ever since then she's been Mother Balfe's spiritual guide."

Margaret Balfe moves out into the hall and closes the doors to the room where the old woman is sleeping.

"Well," she says, that tremulous smile on her lips, "I feel so much better knowing Jill has been in touch with Ardell and is waiting for us to find her."

Good Christ, she has to know her mother-in-law is a hysteric and that voice thing is just some kind of mimic trick she's learned to do. If she doesn't know it, that makes her and the old woman a couple of closet schizoids.

There's a moment of awkward silence there in the hall before Margaret Balfe says, "Oh, about your fee, Mr. Spanner." She pulls a check from her pocket and holds it out. "You said you charged one hundred and fifty dollars a day. This is for one thousand, fifty dollars, a week in advance. Is that satisfactory?"

"It'll do. Thank you. I'll let you hear as soon as I know anything. Oh, and you can do me one favor: will you please call those two girls—Jill's roommates—tell them that you've hired me, and that I'd like to talk to them. Maybe I'll try to see them even later today."

She nods and unchains and opens the door.

Outside on the street, the air is glazed with heat and heavily scented with the gaseous residue of the city's usual unhealthy high accumulation of nitrogen oxide. But it has never smelled better.

> ... Two sections of New York City's health and administrative codes prohibit the dumping of litter, garbage, cans, ashes, rubbish or broken glass onto sidewalks, streets, areaways, yards, lots, or other public places. Violators can be fined from $10 to a maximum of $25 per offense ...

THERE is a shiny new Pontiac Ventura police cruiser parked lopsided in front of the entrance to the 16th Precinct, in the West Forties in Manhattan; the car's right rear wheel resting in a pothole in the pavement the size of a small bomb crater.

The station house is an ugly three-story building worn and blackened by time and the weather which probably never looked like much even when it was first put up God knows how many years earlier. It's set in the middle of a neighborhood of tenements where up and down the street busted bags of garbage have spilled out from the sidewalk into the gutter. At 2:00 P.M., with the temperature at 88°, the whole area has a fragrant odor and is swarming with big black flies.

Inside the station house, it's busy around the booking desk where the sergeant is writing reports on three prisoners in handcuffs who are in the custody of seven plainclothesmen.

The Missing Persons Bureau is on the second floor. The elevator is in the back of the building, but it's being used somewhere on an upper floor, and it's faster to use the stairs.

On the second floor, the door to Room 201 has a frosted glass panel on which some of the lettering is chipped away so it reads: MIS ING P RSONS.

Inside is a long, narrow space lit by overhead fluorescent tubing. The walls are off-white, and the wooden floor is bare. There is a low railing with swing gates a few feet inside the door, separating the entranceway from the rest of the room. Behind the railing is a row of desks and behind one of the desks, the desk nearest the railing, is a plainclothesman, eating a sandwich. Beyond the desks are a couple of enclosed cubicles at the front of the building.

The plainclothesman is a stocky man far enough along in age to be able to calculate the days to his mandatory retirement. His face is puffy, his complexion a sallow white except for a fiery splotch of razor burn under the jaw, and the crown of his bald head is sprinkled with brownish liver spots. He's wearing a Glenurquhart plaid suit with chalk stripes on navy, a wide tie with red circles on a blue background, and a white shirt with a wilted collar.

He glances across the railing, chewing his sandwich. "Help ya?"

"Sergeant Hornstein here? He's expecting me. I just talked to him on the phone. The name's Spanner."

"Yeah," he says, and he yells out toward the other end of the room, "Hey, Sarge! Somebody to see ya."

A man appears at the doorway to one of the cubicles at the front of the building and waves an arm. He waits there to shake hands, introduces himself—"Sergeant Murray Hornstein"—then goes into the cubicle, sits behind his desk, and motions to a chair. It isn't much of an office; the desk, two chairs, a typewriter and table behind him on one side, a five-drawer steel filing cabinet on the other side. There's a pile of bulging file folders stacked up on top of the cabinet, more file folders on the floor and scattered across his desk. There's a half-eaten tuna sandwich on the desk and a cup of black coffee. Venetian blinds cover the cubicle's one window, which looks out the front of the station house.

"You might want to see my I.D., sergeant."

"Uh—right." He glances quickly but carefully at the private investigator's license and pushes it back across the desk.

Murray Hornstein is near fifty, not too tall but solidly built, with broad shoulders and a muscular torso. His hair is wiry gray, clipped short, and his face has a scrubbed glow to it, the way skin sometimes shines after washing with soap and cold water. He wears glasses with thick black frames. His brown and white seersucker jacket is draped over the back of his chair and he's wearing a white shirt with short sleeves and a lemony yellow bow tie. It's not hard to imagine him as the favorite uncle of some Hewlett, Long Island, Jewish Princess.

"J. T. Spanner," he says, his voice curious. "When you called on the phone, the name sounded familiar. Do I know you from someplace? I mean, besides the fact that I know you were the one who found that body on the bridge this morning."

"It's possible. I used to be on the force myself. In fact, my last assignment was here at the one-six. In Homicide."

Hornstein smacks his forehead with the palm of his open hand. "Of course! I remember now. I never knew you, but I know the name. You left about six, seven years ago. Am I right?"

"More like ten, eleven years ago."

Hornstein grimaces. "*That* long. Where the hell does it go, time? Ten, eleven years ago—let's see, that makes it you worked under Max Kauffman in Homicide. Am I right? Did you know he's a deputy chief inspector now, and the precinct commander?"

"Yeah, I know. The inspector and I have been in touch from time to time."

"Is that so?" He picks up his cup. "Like some coffee? We've always got a pot brewing in the other office."

"No, thanks. I had lunch on the way here."

"Tell me," he asks; "you ever miss the force, worry about giving up your pension?"

"Sometimes, sure. But, well, I've done all right, more or less, though it's kept me hustling."

Hornstein makes a placating gesture with his hand. "Not that it's any of my business, but can you make a decent living in private investigation work? I mean I'm just curious."

"I don't mind telling you. Like I said, you hustle, you can. An average of—oh, say, the upper twenty thousands per year."

"Is that so?" Hornstein leans back in his chair, holding his cup. "Well, now, when you phoned, you said you wanted to talk about this Jill Balfe, who's reported missing. What can I do for you?"

"I just got involved this morning. Mrs. Balfe—the mother—has hired me to help look for Jill. She got my name when she heard from the police that I was the one who found the body on the bridge this morning. I was up there in the Bronx getting some background from her earlier. She told me she was in touch with you. I wanted you to know I was on the case. I wondered if you had any leads, any information, any theories, you might not have told Mrs. Balfe and that you'd share with me."

Hornstein takes a sip of coffee, puts the cup down, and rubs the side of his nose with a finger. "I feel sorry for that woman—Mrs. Balfe. Hell, I don't even know for sure anything's happened to her daughter."

"Then you don't think the body the police had earlier was Jill Balfe's?"

"Uh—I didn't say that. I've got no proof, one way or the other. Neither has Homicide."

"Still, wouldn't you say if it wasn't her body, her disappearance around the same time and in the same general area would have to be one hell of a coincidence?"

"A coincidence. So?" He shrugs his shoulders. "Coincidences happen. You know as well as I do in this city some people are always getting murdered and some other people are always disappearing. Am I right?"

"Even so—"

Hornstein raises a hand to interrupt. "Look, Spanner, I'm not trying to jerk you around. Of course, we *suspect* the dead girl was Jill Balfe. But proof—we got none. What I'm trying to indicate to you is our minds are not closed on the subject. We're still handling them as two separate cases. I've got one, Homicide's got the other. Let me show you something."

He leans down and picks up a file folder from the floor. The folder's stuffed with about an inch-thick stack of papers. He puts the folder on his desk and flips it open. "This is the information I've accumulated on her so far." He holds up a photograph of Jill Balfe in her stewardess's uniform. "You got a picture of her?"

"Yeah, it looks like the same one you have."

"All right, let's review what we've found out so far." He shuffles through the papers. "We've really been wearing out the shoe leather on this one since early morning. By the time we saw the teletype from the Bronx that Mrs. Balfe called to say her daughter was missing, we had the report on the unidentified body which had been found and stolen although it took a few hours to hook up the possible connection. Normally, we wouldn't check on a reported missing person this quick. When we started our investigation into her disappearance, we concentrated on tracking down witnesses who might have seen her when she arrived at JFK Airport."

Hornstein glances up. "I guess you heard most of this before, from the mother, but I want to fill you in on what the department knows and doesn't know."

"I appreciate that, sergeant."

Hornstein nods. "We found three people who saw her

in the airlines terminal after the flight got in, but she didn't check in at her office there as she was supposed to do. Just so you'll have the names, the three witnesses who saw her that night are Captain Joseph Shanley, pilot of the plane she flew in on, who works for U.S.-Global Airlines, the same outfit she worked for; and two stewardesses from another airline, Pan Am, who knew Jill. The two stewardesses are a Jennifer Kupperton and a Lillian Holm. She was never seen after that."

Hornstein pauses and clears his throat. "You got all that?"

"I've got it."

Hornstein flips over a couple of papers in the file. "I don't have to tell you that the possibility that she might have been the dead girl we found and lost has made this more than just a routine missing-persons. We've really sweated this one in just the few hours that have passed. Every available man in the precinct's been out working on the case."

Hornstein pauses and rubs his chin. "You talked to her mother, you heard what she has to say about Jill; an average happy-go-lucky girl who never gave anybody any trouble?"

"So she said."

Hornstein pats the stack of papers. "Everybody else in this file says the same thing."

The sergeant shifts his body in the chair and frowns. "Now we come to the only oddity in the case. A guy named Duane Vinton. He was one of the guys Jill dated."

"Yeah? And—?"

"You haven't visited the building where Jill lived, yet, have you?"

"No. I plan to drop over when I finish here."

"It's one of those fancy high-rises," Hornstein says. "And in the basement they've got this health club. Health spa. The Good Health Spa, they call it. Cute. Sauna baths, exercise rooms, even a swimming pool. You know the kind of place, for people with money—and fat—to burn. Jill and her roommates used to go there. This Duane Vinton was the assistant manager of the place; that's how Jill met him. And they dated, although there's nothing to indicate it was any big thing."

"You said he *was* the assistant manager. What's that mean?"

A nerve twitches in Hornstein's right cheek. "He's disappeared, too. About a week ago, we hear." He's silent for a moment. He shrugs. "It may not mean a damn thing."

"Come on, sergeant! Come on! What do you mean it may not mean a damn thing?"

"Aha!" Hornstein says smugly and points a finger across the desk. "Now you've got your answer as to why we've tried to keep an open mind about the case. You've jumped to the conclusion they've gone off together. Which is a possibility we have to consider, too. However, you see, there could be another explanation for his disappearance; one that has nothing to do with Jill Balfe."

"Like what?"

"Like the fact that he's a full-time hustler, and a two-bit one at that. One of those physically well-set-up jock types with all his brains and his morals in his balls who, wouldn't you know, totalizes all the pussy in sight—reports have it there's more than he can handle flips out over him, always to their everlasting physical, emotional and, most especially, financial regret. A guy like that—things must have a way of heating up for him. Now and then he must have a need to get lost temporarily, to cool a situation. We hear it's happened before."

"Does he live in the same apartment building?"

Hornstein smiles tightly. "Not this schmuck. He lives at the Seventy-ninth Street Marina, over in the Hudson River. On a houseboat, no less. I haven't personally been inside it, but they say it's a fucking floating make-out pad with wall-to-wall everything. Ah, well."

Hornstein takes a swig of coffee and sets the empty cup on the desk. "Like I said, it's the only disturbing element we've run across in the case. And his disappearance probably doesn't have any connection with hers. In fact, Vinton's not even officially listed as missing. Unofficially, we're keeping an eye out for him, though. You understand this whole business about Vinton is confidential?"

"Understood. Jill's mother doesn't know about him, does she?"

"No. There's really nothing to tell her, am I right? I've been talking to you cop-to-cop, more or less."

Hornstein thinks for a moment. "Look, you want to talk to Captain Tynan in Homicide while you're here? He's handling the case of the body that disappeared. You want me to see if he's in?"

"Yeah, sure."

"Wait here."

Hornstein leaves the office and is gone for about five or six minutes. When he returns, he's carrying a manila envelope. "The captain's out," he says. "But I thought you might want to see the pictures they shot of the body last night."

Hornstein perches on the edge of the desk and spreads a dozen photographs out in front of him. "Not pretty, huh?"

Although shot from different angles, the corpse is the same in every photograph: the body like a stark marble sculpture of human suffering.

"You can see why nobody—not even a mother trying to recognize her daughter—could make an I.D. from these photographs."

"Yeah."

Hornstein points a finger at the photos on the desk. "The lab boys did all their numbers on these. Blow-ups, microscopic scans, what-have-you, and all they got was larger and smaller shots of what you can see here. Nothing to give us a possible lead to why the body was heisted."

"That still the official theory of why the body was stolen? Because some mark or evidence had been left on it which could be incriminating to the perpetrators?"

"That's one of the theories," Hornstein says. "There's another possibility. Which is somebody wanted to prevent a positive identification of the corpse. If so, they fucking well accomplished it."

"It's as messy a sight as I've ever seen."

Hornstein nods his head, his expression dour. "And I've seen the work of a lot of perverts in my time."

"What about the guys on the morgue wagon? They couldn't supply you with any clues to who stole the body or to the car that forced them off the road?"

Hornstein shakes his head disgustedly. "A couple of klutzes. My guess is they were so afraid they were going to get their asses shot off that they didn't register anything. They couldn't even agree on descriptions of the perpetrators. One guy said they were both tall; the other said they were both short. And the best they could do on the car was that it was a Toyota and looked fairly new. Of course, who would ever expect a morgue wagon to be hijacked?"

"If the body wasn't Jill Balfe's, have you got any other candidates?"

"A good question. And I do have the answer for you." Hornstein pulls a sheet of paper from the file folder. "This is a list we did of all persons officially reported missing in the city within the past forty-eight hours. In Manhattan and the other four boroughs, the total came to seventy-five. Of that number, thirty female subjects are still unaccounted for; and of that number, at least nineteen fit the estimated age-range, height, weight, and hair coloring of the victim in the photographs. You can see the dimensions of the problem?"

"Clearly. All too clearly."

He closes the file. "Well, that's it. Now you know everything we know. Any other questions?"

"I can't think of any."

"So, then, I wish you good luck."

"Thanks. And thanks again for your time, sergeant. Be seeing you."

"See you. So long, Spanner."

Hornstein picks up the photographs carefully, one by one, stacks them together, and slides them back into the envelope. Hornstein doesn't look up again. He's not even aware that he's being observed as, a moment later, he takes the photographs out once more and looks at them, his face troubled. Although he probably wouldn't want anyone to know it, he looks like the kind of guy who takes it personally that people are missing or misplaced or murdered.

> ... According to the last census taken,
> there are 67,000–plus people for each
> square mile of New York City ...

"HEY!" Bobbie Gillian says. "You know what? You're the first real private eye I've ever seen. Did anybody ever tell you you look like a cop?"

She pads barefoot across the thick white carpeting of the apartment's foyer and on into the living room, saying, "I must look a mess. I was in the middle of washing my hair when you phoned."

"Yeah, well, I've been calling here all afternoon. I was about ready to give it up for the day and then you answered."

"Mrs. Balfe called and said you'd probably be by to talk about Jill. You're the one that found that body on the bridge this morning."

"That's me."

Standing in the living room, she says, "Come on in."

It's a large L-shaped room, decorated in career-girl mod. A lot of chrome, a lot of glass. Six or seven Mies van der Rohe-type chairs with chrome frames and chrome legs, a coffee table and two end tables of chrome-and-glass—probably Brancusis—a lot of hokey Art Deco prints and smoky glass mirrors hanging about, a loveseat and a long, curving sofa, both in satiny ivory. A lot of throw pillows of red satin and some of them shaped like hearts, on the sofa, on the loveseat, on the chairs, and on the floor.

The windows have vertical blinds. The drapes are white and so are the walls, and so is the expanse of thick carpeting which begins inside the door in the foyer and spreads out over every square foot of floor in sight in the apartment. There's soft music in the background from a couple of stereo speakers concealed somewhere on either side of the room. The temperature must be air-conditioned 25° cooler than on the street. Sunset is still an hour away by the clock, but outside the windows the sky, overcast and darkening hour by hour through the afternoon, is now black with thunderclouds. In the half-shadows of the false twilight there's a kind of day's-end stillness in the air. Soon it will rain.

On the coffee table in front of the sofa there's a tall, frosted glass filled with crushed ice and a colorless liquid with a lime peel floating on top.

Bobbie Gillian sits on the sofa within reach of the glass and flicks a hand in the direction of one of the chrome-legged chairs on the opposite side of the coffee table. "Grab a seat. Fix you a drink? I'm having a gin and tonic." She makes a move to rise again.

"No, that's okay. Thanks. Maybe I can take a rain check, though."

She nods and tucks her bare legs under her. She's wearing a fluffy pink terry-cloth wrap-around. Her head is covered, turban-style, by a towel and some of her hair is showing, burnished blonde, under the edges of the towel. She's in her late twenties—not tall, five feet, maybe three, four inches in height—and from what can be seen where the wrap-around doesn't quite wrap around is rounded and curved in the right places. Her face just misses being beautiful by a nose that's too short and that gives her, instead, a pixie-pretty look. She seems totally unaware that there is about her an aura of smoldering sexuality, the appeal of a sleeping libido waiting to be awakened.

"I'm sorry no one was here earlier," she says. "After Jill's mother phoned and said you were working for her and would probably want to talk to us, I had to go shopping, and Karen—my roommate, Karen Rushler—had an appointment with the hairdresser. She should be back soon, so maybe you'll still get to see her today."

"Good. I had hoped to talk to both of you about Jill."

"What can I do to help?"

"Well, for openers, I'd like to have your impression of Jill. It'll be off the record, just whatever you can tell me about her."

Bobbie Gillian frowns. "I've always liked her. Most people seem to. She's not hard to get along with. At first, when she moved in with us, about three years ago, she seemed reserved, a little stiff. But she's loosened up since then. I think it was because she'd always lived at home before."

"How did she happen to move in with you and your roommate?"

She shrugs. "Karen and I have been roommates for about five years. There was another girl living with us before. Then she got married around the time Jill first went to work for U.S.-Global. Karen met Jill first and then—I don't know—either Jill heard we were looking for a new roommate, or Karen heard Jill was looking for a place to live. Anyhow, we all seemed to hit it off, and Jill moved in."

"Would you call her a dependable person?"

"Jill? Gee, yes. Anything but flaky. In fact, sometimes, a little too uptight. Naïve, almost. I think she had a kind of strict religious upbringing. You met her mother. After a while, Jill learned to swing some, though."

"Define 'swing some' for me."

"Uh"—her eyebrows lift—"you know, dates, a little fun, like that."

"I understand she frequently double-dated with you or your roommate."

"She did," Bobbie Gillian says. "That's right. Generally, whenever any two of us were off duty at the same time, we went out together with our dates, and sometimes all three of us and our dates went out together."

"Did you usually go with the same guys?"

"Sometimes yes, sometimes no."

"I mean Jill—did she usually go out with one guy more often than another?"

She shakes her head. "I wouldn't say 'usually.' I mean, as far as I know, none of us is looking for any kind of permanent arrangement. They're just guys, dates, for drinks, dinner, maybe to listen to some music. At P.J.'s, Maxwell's Plum, the Rainbow Room, Dangerfield's, like that." She leans forward and picks up the glass of gin and tonic from the coffee table.

"How about this fellow—Duane Vinton—from the health club downstairs? Was there anything between Jill and him, do you think?"

She takes a sip of her drink before she answers. "She dated him a few times or so. We all know Duane, from going to the health spa. But as far as anything uh—more—between them, you couldn't prove it by me."

"You do know he's missing, too, don't you?"

She nods. "I'd heard he hadn't been around, yes."

"You don't think there's any connection with that and Jill's disappearance?"

"The police have been here all morning asking the same question. I can't think of why there should be any connection, and neither can Karen."

"And you can't think of any other reason why Jill would want to cut out for a while?"

"No. None. And besides that, she didn't take any of her things. Everything in her room is just like she left it before she went on the flight to Belgium. That doesn't make sense if she'd planned to disappear."

She leans forward and puts her glass down on the coffee table. She gives a shiver as she says, "All this stuff is kind of scary, you know. I mean the police coming around, the questions, all that stuff about the body they found, and was it Jill, and all. The police had Karen and me look at the pictures they took of that body to see if we thought it was Jill. You've seen them? I ask you: how could anybody ever tell who that was? I try not to think about it."

She's silent for a moment. Outside the windows, bolts of blue-white lightning suddenly whipsnap across the black sky with an explosive crackling of thunder and the rain comes down in a cloudburst.

Bobbie Gillian jumps as if she's been goosed and says with a shaky laugh, "Wow! That almost scared me out of my skin!"

"It should cool things off now."

She takes a couple of swallows of her drink and looks over the rim of the glass. "Can I ask you something, Mr. Spanner?"

"Sure."

"Do you think Jill's dead?"

"I don't know. Do you think so?"

She makes a meaningless gesture with one hand while she sets the drink down on the coffee table with the other hand. "Sometimes I do and sometimes I don't. I don't like to think she's dead but then I think, if she isn't dead, where is she? Other times I think maybe the whole thing's just a misunderstanding and one day soon she'll pop up again with a perfectly logical explanation for her absence."

"It could happen."

"Can I ask you something else?"

"Sure."

"If she is dead, do you think you'll be able to find out what happened?"

"Not likely, no. The police are better equipped for work like that."

She arches an eyebrow. "You know what I've observed about you, Mr. Spanner?"

"No. What's that?"

She smiles. "You ask questions better than you answer them. All this time we've talked and you've found out a lot about me and I know absolutely nothing about you."

"What did you have in mind that you wanted to know?"

"Like"—she flounders for a moment—"is it interesting being a private eye?"

"Sometimes. The rest of the time it's routine, security work, recovering stolen property, once in a while working as a bodyguard, now and then a divorce case—although those I try to avoid unless I'm really strapped for dough. It's a living, if you stay busy."

She smiles again. "You still haven't told me anything about yourself. About *you*."

"Oh, you mean personally? Let's see, I'm thirty-eight years old. I went with the police department right out of college and had made detective by the time I resigned from the force ten, eleven years ago. Oh, yeah, and I'm unmarried—twice."

Bobbie Gillian looks flustered for a moment. She starts to say something but before she can get the words out there's the sound of a key in the door. Startled, she jumps again. "That must be Karen."

The door closes and a tall, leggy redhead walks into the room.

"This is Karen Rushler," Bobbie Gillian says. "Karen, meet J. T. Spanner."

Karen Rushler sticks out a hand. "Hi."

"Hi."

"Want a drink, Karen?" Bobbie Gillian asks.

Karen Rushler nods. "You said the magic word. Scotch, please, love."

Bobbie Gillian glances around. "Sure you won't change your mind, Mr. Spanner?"

"Another time, thanks. I'm going to be shoving off shortly."

Bobbie Gillian disappears into the back of the apartment.

"You spend half a day at the hairdresser's," Karen Rushler says, "and then emerge into the worst storm of the summer." She wrinkles her nose. "I ask you: how do you suppose the elements always know just when to open up and crap on you?" She laughs and takes off the plastic scarf covering her head.

"I'd say, from what I can see, that you've weathered the weather nicely."

She winks. "Actually I had a cab from door to door. But it's more fun to bitch."

She plops down on the sofa. She's dressed in a paisley blouse, cream-colored tailored slacks, fit snug, and beige sandals. The blouse has a floppy collar, long sleeves buttoned at the cuffs, and is open down the front almost to her midriff. Where the fabric of her blouse is stretched tight across her breasts, it makes it obvious she's wearing no bra. She's draped with jewelry; a gold necklace that has a pendant dangling from it, gold bangle bracelets encircling both wrists, rings on the first three fingers of her right hand and the middle and little finger of her left hand.

She's a couple of years older than Bobbie Gillian and several inches taller. Her hair is a rich auburn shade, short against her head with about a half-inch fringe across the forehead. She has wide-set green eyes, a long, elegant nose, and a strong, well-formed mouth and chin.

Beneath her carefully arranged exterior there's a hint of icy hauteur that could probably make a eunuch out of a brass monkey.

She leans forward and takes a cigarette from a lucite

box on the coffee table. Whiffs of her scent—one of the Chanel numbers—drift in the air. In the silence while she lights the cigarette, the taut, drumming sound of the rain against the windows is like a muted background beat for the soft music coming from the stereo. Intermittent flashes of lightning, now far off, still flicker in the darkness outside the windows.

Karen Rushler exhales a small plume of smoke. "I have a reputation for being very blunt, Mr. Spanner. When I spoke with Mrs. Balfe on the phone earlier, she seemed so pathetic that I agreed to talk to you. But I think you should know that I didn't really want to see you."

"Oh? And why's that?"

"Because," she says, "this endless discussion of Jill seems pointless to me. I mean, sure, I feel sorry about the poor kid, whatever's become of her. But"—she tosses her head back and the expression on her face is one of distaste—"I don't think you or anyone else can appreciate what a sordid nightmare this morning has been. The police, the vulgar publicity, the endless interrogations, the—the feeling—the—sense—of—violation—of my personal privacy being invaded—not to mention other—other incidents that have been going on for the past week."

She pauses and sits up very straight on the sofa. "The fact is, whatever happened, it has nothing to do with me, and I'm sick of talking about it and hearing about it. You can think me selfish, but that's the way I feel."

"Look, I think I can appreciate your feelings. You're only human and it's not selfish to think the way you do."

"You really believe that?"

"Yeah. I do. But forget Jill Balfe for the moment. I'm interested in something else you said, something about 'other incidents.' Miss Gillian didn't mention anything like that. You want to tell me?"

Before she can answer, Bobbie Gillian comes back into the room, carrying a glass. "Did I hear someone taking my

50

name in vain?" she asks. She hands Karen Rushler the drink, then sits down beside her on the sofa.

"Thanks, Bobbie," Karen Rushler says. She takes a sip of the scotch and says to Bobbie Gillian, "I was just getting ready to tell Mr. Spanner about the things that happened around here the last week or so or that we *think* happened. He says you didn't say anything about them."

Bobbie Gillian makes a wry face. "Oh, God, *that?* I didn't say anything about them because I was afraid he'd get the impression that we were a couple of kooks."

"Well, I'm going to tell him anyhow," Karen Rushler says. She stubs her cigarette out in an ashtray on the coffee table and looks up. "We can't prove it but we think that, during the times we were both away from the apartment in the last week or so, somebody came in here and searched the place. There's no evidence. Nothing was taken. But little things seemed to be slightly out of place. Bobbie and I both noticed it, independently of one another. And every time it happened, it was when we'd both been away at the same time on a flight for two or three days. Jill didn't seem to notice it and shrugged it off. Also, there was a period when Bobbie and I believed we were being followed and watched. Again—separately—each of us caught glimpses of the man following us."

"Do you think it was the same man watching each of you?"

They both nod and Karen Rushler says, "He was a big man. And he always seemed to be dressed in dark clothing. Sometimes one or the other of us would spot him outside the apartment building, or at various times and places when we'd be somewhere else in town."

"Have you informed the police about these incidents?"

They both shake their heads. "Frankly," Karen Rushler says, "I thought it would only give them more excuses to pry into our affairs. And we had no proof."

"I suppose it's foolish to think the security in the building isn't that good, even with the doormen downstairs and the elevator operators?"

"Let's just say there have been several robberies and one unsolved murder in the building since we've lived here," Karen Rushler says. "I imagine that's about the way it is in any place in Manhattan today. If somebody wants to get in, they'll get in."

"Well, I'll tell you what: if you have any suspicions, any time again, that any of these incidents are taking place, let me know immediately. Then I'll see what I can do to help. Here's one of my cards for each of you."

Karen Rushler glances up from looking at the card she's taken in her hand. "I'm afraid I came on kind of tight-assed with you earlier, Mr. Spanner. About Jill, I mean. Bobbie's probably given you the full rundown on her already, anyway. We've both recited it so often we can do it by rote by now. But I'd like you to know that if you have any questions you want to ask me about Jill, I'll try to answer."

"Thank you, Miss Rushler. Actually there are only two. Miss Gillian has given me her answers but I'd like yours."

"Ask away."

"First, as you know, this fellow, Duane Vinton, has dropped out of sight, too. Do you think it had anything to do with Jill's disappearance?"

"Oh, there was something between Jill and Duane, no doubt about it. I think she was impressionable and had a crush on him. Which was not reciprocated, I don't think. But I can't see where it would make any sense at all that they'd just go off without a word to anybody. So my answer is no."

"Okay. Second question: do you have any idea at all why Jill might choose to vanish on her own?"

"I don't." Karen Rushler shakes her head. "But I suppose anything's possible." She half-smiles. "Not much help, huh? That's one of the problems Bobbie and I have had all along."

"Just to know what your opinions are is a help."

"And that's all you want to ask me?"

"Unless you have something else to add, that's all."

"I can't think of a thing." She stands. "I hope you'll excuse me now. I have a date and I'd better start getting ready."

"Yeah. I'm leaving, too."

Her handshake is firm and she leaves lingering traces of Chanel floating behind as she goes out of the room.

"You're going to get soaked out there tonight," Bobbie Gillian says, looking at the rain splattering against the windows.

"I'll be all right. My car's parked almost at the door."

"I'll walk you to the elevator," she says, moving ahead to the front door in the foyer. She walks along on into the hall, saying, "I notice your office is right near Forty-second Street on Lexington. I know the building—the Graybar. I'm in that area a lot."

"Sometime when you are, why don't you drop by and see me? Maybe we can have lunch or I'll take you up on that rain check for a drink."

"I'll keep it in mind."

The elevator comes. She runs the tip of her pink tongue playfully, sensually, over her lips as her mouth forms a parting smile.

That makes it a total of two rain checks for the day.

> NO SMOKING
> IN ELEVATORS
> UNDER PENALTY
> OF LAW
>
> ———*Sign in elevator at 600 East 38th Street*

DOWNSTAIRS, the building's lobby looks as though it belongs in some Collins Avenue, Miami Beach hotel. Sparkling crystal chandeliers hang in clusters from the two-story-high ceiling, the floor is marble overlaid down the center with red carpeting, and both sides of the lobby are lined in rosewood paneling. There are rosewood benches set here and there around the lobby. This is the chic East Side of Manhattan, so of course they have what they call a concierge desk and a uniformed attendant on duty behind it. There's another uniformed attendant stationed in front of the bank of elevators across from the desk, and at the front of the lobby a uniformed doorman busy beyond the double plate-glass doors where several taxicabs have pulled up with people arriving at the building. Outside, there's a zebra-striped canopy strung across the front of the entrance. Rain is gusting in sheets all up and down the street, and the canopy is billowing in the wind.

It's only about seven or eight paces from the end of the canopy to where the T-Bird is parked at the curb. The rain is pelting down, bouncing off the pavement and running in rivulets across the sidewalk and into the gutters.

After being closed up, the air inside the car is stale, humid, and the seats and steering wheel are sticky-damp to the touch. The car is parked in front of the east end of the building where Jill Balfe lived. There's a second, smaller canopy there and through the blur of rain streaming down the outside of the car windows, it's possible to make out the words GOOD HEALTH SPA printed across the top of the canopy which is over a doorway set several steps below street level.

The heavy rain has slowed traffic to a crawl on East 38th Street, in the direction of First Avenue. There's barely room to swing the T-Bird out into the street and squeeze it in behind a taxi and in front of a car which has pulled out at the same time a couple of doors down the block. Another taxi, passing on the opposite side of the street, sprays the side of the T-Bird with a cascade of water from the overflowing sewers. It's stop-and-go, stop-and-go, all the way to the corner.

Finally, around the corner on First Avenue traveling north, uptown, traffic moves faster. In the darkness, to the west, the lights of the city's skyscrapers high above the avenue form a giant frosted mosaic behind the translucent screen of rain. A few blocks farther on, at 42nd Street, when the United Nations Building comes into view, the car phone buzzes. It's Ellie calling from the office.

"I just wanted to tell you I'm closing up for the night. Nothing new here," she says. "How are you doing on the case?"

"I just left the apartment where Jill Balfe lived. I had a talk with her two roommates. Before that, I saw Jill's mother and a Sergeant Hornstein at the One-six Precinct, who's in charge of the case. About all I have to report so far is her disappearance is a puzzler to everybody."

"You didn't pick up anything from the police that they hadn't told Mrs. Balfe?"

"Only that there was some character Jill dated now and then, and he disappeared, too, about a week before she did. Nobody—including the police—seems to think it means anything. I'm not so sure. Another odd angle is that, according to Jill's roommates, some peculiar things have been going on at the apartment for the last week or so. They think the place was searched at various times while they were both away, and that at least for a while there was a tail on them—the same man watching both of them."

"Hang on a minute," Ellie says, her voice drifting away.

The rain is beginning to slacken a bit, and traffic is thinning out along First Avenue. Up ahead, at the corner, is 52nd Street. East of First, 52nd is only one block long, coming to a dead end up above the FDR Drive and the East River, which are now shrouded in the misty rain. There are not too many cars parked on the street, and it's easy to find a spot where the T-Bird will fit in the middle of the block. Up at the corner, another car turns into 52nd, a car whose mismatching headlights—one bright and the other, the left headlight, dim—are framed in the T-Bird's rearview mirror.

Ellie's voice comes back on the line. "Sorry, J. T., Lee just called. She said to tell you hello."

"Hold it a minute, Ellie. I just noticed something. Sonofabitch, I'm being tailed."

"Tailed?" Ellie asks. "Are you sure? Where are you?"

"I'm parked on Fifty-second Street, east of First. I'm on my way to eat at Billy's Restaurant, at the corner. I didn't realize until now that ever since I left that apartment building I've been picking up the headlights of the same car in my rearview mirror. Now whoever it is has turned in here to Fifty-second Street, too, and is parking down at the end of the block."

"You watch it now, J. T., you hear?" Ellie says.

"I'll talk to you tomorrow, honey."

The headlights go off on the car that has parked down the street but nobody gets out.

Back on the corner of First Avenue, there's a florist shop which has a large awning outside. It looks like a good spot from which to observe the car down the street. Billy's Restaurant is next door to the florist shop.

There's nobody in sight on the streets around. There's a fine drizzle coming down and a strong wind is blowing in from the East River. The street lights along the block are ringed by vapor halos.

From under the awning, there's a clear view of the dark car. Almost immediately a man gets out of the car. He comes along the block, head down, walking fast. In Karen Rushler's words, he is a big man, and he's wearing a black raincoat. He comes around the corner, under the awning, and stops suddenly in surprise. For a moment, he's immobile, eyes fixed on the barrel of the S&W .357 Magnum poking into his belly. Then his head jerks up.

"For God's sake," he says hoarsely, "don't do anything foolish. I can explain—"

"Who are you? Why are you following me?"

Sweat pops out on his face, visible in the light from the florist's window. "Listen," he says, talking rapidly, "I'm a detective, too, private, like you. Honest to Christ. We're both working the same case, in a way. Show you my license."

"You carrying a gun?"

He nods and inclines his head to the left side. "It's under my arm."

"Let's see it. Keep it in sight. But don't touch it."

He fumbles hastily with the buttons of his raincoat and yanks it and his suit coat open. Underneath he's wearing a shoulder harness and there's the butt of a revolver sticking out of the holster.

"Now let's see some I.D."

His right hand dips into the side pocket of his suit coat and comes out holding a black leather billfold. He flips the billfold open and holds the license up to the light. The license identifies him as Harry Flescher of the Trans-America Security Agency, New York City, and is stamped and signed by the New York Secretary of State.

"Uh-huh, you're a detective like me, all right. But that doesn't explain why you were following me."

He sighs wearily. "Jesus, this is going to sound dumb. I just wanted to talk to you. I was tailing you to see if you were meeting anyone before I made my approach. That's the fact of the matter."

"About this same case we're both supposed to be working on—if we are—what's your angle?"

"I have been hired to find this guy, Duane Vinton," Flescher says. "I know you know who he is."

"Yeah? How do you know so much about what I know?"

He shifts his weight from one foot to the other. "Like I said, I can explain it. But what the fuck, can't we find somewhere better than out here in the street to talk? Besides, I got to take a leak."

"I was headed for Billy's, next door there—"

"Great, great," he says enthusiastically. "Let's talk inside."

The front of Billy's Bar and Restaurant has two large windows looking out on First Avenue, about evenly divided on either side of the front door. Inside that door are two swinging doors. Flescher ducks quickly inside the outer door and holds one of the swinging doors open.

The place is almost completely filled with customers, as usual, even on this rainy night. The atmosphere inside is that of a pleasant intimate pub. There's a hexagonal tile floor sprinkled with sawdust. To the right of the swinging doors is a long bar of rich African mahogany extending half the length of the room. The bar is backed by mirrors in front of which are rows of bottles. Most of the wall space is paneled in dark wood, and some of the lighting comes from authentic gaslight globes hanging from brass fixtures. The several dozen tables all have red-checkered cloths. On the wall, at various spots around the room, are square plaques of dark wood on which the restaurant's menu is lettered in gold. Approximately midway down the room is a low-hanging beam with a large plaque attached to it which reads:

Established By MICHAEL CONDRON
Way Back in 1870

Flescher heads for an empty table in the front part of the room across from the bar. He doesn't sit down. He stands by the table and says, "Order me a drink, huh? A double Cutty Sark on the rocks. Be right back." He heads quickly for the men's room.

One of the waiters comes over to the table.

"We'll have a couple of drinks. A double Cutty Sark on the rocks, a double Jack Daniel's and water."

The waiter nods and goes away.

The rain has started to come down hard again outside. An opaque film of moisture forms on the windows so there's a feeling that the restaurant is sealed off from the night and the rest of the world.

Harry Flescher gets back to the table just as the waiter brings the drinks. Flescher drapes his black raincoat over one of the chairs and then sits in a chair on the opposite side of the table, with his back to the door.

"This place is okay," he says, looking around and nodding his head. He lifts his glass in the gesture of a toast.

He's a large man, over six feet tall, and has a big-boned frame. He must be sixty years old. There's not much of his still-dark hair left, and it lies plastered to his head like black stripes painted across the top of the bony skull. His dark eyes are set in shadowed hollows under bushy black brows. Below his chin, his face has dissolved into wattled flesh.

He leans back in his chair and digs a loose cigarette out of the pocket of his rumpled blue suit. "Days like this, I begin to think maybe I'm getting too old for the business," he says. "The way you pegged me tailing you, and then I walk blindly right into your gun. If you had been somebody who wanted to kill me, I'd be dead. You know?"

"Okay, Flescher, let's cut out all the bullshit. I want some answers from you. How you know about me. How you happened to be able to pick me up and tail me from Thirty-eighth Street."

"Fair enough." He hunches his body halfway across the table and says in a low voice: "I got that apartment where those two girls live bugged. In my car is a Sony AM/FM cassette recorder adapted to receive sounds transmitted by a bug so small it's hidden behind an electric wall socket in their living room. When my car is parked outside that building, nobody picks their nose in that room that I can't hear it. I was listening in today while you were there."

"You must be out of your fucking gourd, Flescher. The law catches you bugging and they'll put you away for a five-to-ten."

He shakes his head. "They're not going to catch me." He gulps down most of the scotch in his glass.

"That's what they all say. What about are you also the one who was tailing those two girls for a while?"

"That was me all right. I heard them telling you about that. I knew at the time they'd made me; that's why I quit following them. The reason I been concentrating on that apartment is because Duane Vinton used to date one of the girls—that Jill Balfe—before he disappeared a week or so ago. I been hoping the girls would give me a line to him."

"What about searching their place—was that you, too?"

He lights the cigarette he's been rolling around in his

lips and then waggles a couple of fingers at the waiter. "I heard them telling you about that," he says, "and nope, that wasn't me."

Before he can say anything else, the waiter comes over to the table.

"You want another drink?" Flescher asks. "And how about we order? I'm paying."

"Another double Jack Daniel's. And a steak, rare, baked potato with sour cream, a green salad with oil and vinegar."

"Make that two on the dinners," Flescher tells the waiter, "and bring me another double Cutty on the rocks."

After the waiter leaves, Flescher squints through a puff of smoke from his cigarette and says, "About that rifling the apartment, that honest-to-God wasn't me. But I'll tell you this: from the first I got involved, I've had the feeling there was another party futzing around in this case. But I've never been able to catch them at it."

He finishes off his drink, rattling the ice around in the empty glass. "Tell you something else: whoever this party is, they're good at staying out of sight. I'll give you an example. Sometimes when I have to be someplace else, I leave the car parked in front of that building with the tape recorder running. That way I can hear if there's anything goes on when I'm not there. Well, there's this one time when I ran the tape later—the two girls are talking and are leaving the apartment for a trip. You can hear them go out."

He rattles the ice around some more. "Now it happens, just by accident, I let that tape keep running, and after a while there's the sound of the door opening and somebody's in there, moving around. You can hear them going through the place. At the time I felt it was a man. I saved the tape. I'll play it sometime for you if you say so."

"Maybe I'll take you up on it. But right now something

else is bothering me. That's how did you get into that apartment to plant the bug?"

He grins. "I told the guy on duty at the service entrance I was from the telephone company. The girls were away at the time. I'd already made certain of that. I told the guy it would be a real pain in the anus for me if I couldn't get in and had to come back another time. I flashed a phony I.D. card at him and slipped him some cash. I probably didn't fool him. He didn't care. That's how most of the breaking-and-entering jobs are pulled in this town. The guy left or got fired from there since."

The waiter brings fresh drinks.

Flescher cradles his drink in the palm of his hand. "Now, if you're wondering why I'd tell you all this and risk you blowing the whistle on me, the answers are simple."

He takes a slow sip of his drink, then says, "Number one: I figure a smart operator like you, you'd be quick to see how much I might pick up through the bug that could be useful to you. Number two: I figure I open myself up to you, you'll accept that I'm playing it straight with you and maybe we can cooperate with one another, as long as we're both kind of working the same case."

"Before I answer that, tell me how you know I'll play straight with you?"

He nods his head. "Oh, I checked you out. As soon as you walked into that apartment today and I heard your name. I left the tape recorder running in the car and went to a phone booth at the corner and called a buddy at headquarters. He reports you rate kosher with the cops. That's good enough for me. I figure each of us can use all the help we can get. How about it?"

"I guess it's okay—as long as there's no client conflict involved."

"Naturally," Flescher says quickly, "each of us would protect our client's interest. I don't incidentally think that's going to be a problem."

"Which brings me down to the real nitty-gritty, Flescher—"

The waiter interrupts with the dinners.

Flescher is busy for a moment, cutting into his steak. "You were saying?" he asks.

"Who's your client? Who hired you to look for Duane Vinton?"

"Um," he mumbles, chewing his steak, "You—uh—know I can't divulge that information without checking it out with my client first. But I can tell you this: my client claims to have been involved in a business deal with Vinton. Then Vinton drops out of sight. My client gets worried and hires me to look for him. That's all I know. The only orders I have are to locate Vinton's whereabouts and report back to the client."

"The cops know you're looking for Vinton?"

He shakes his head. "As far as I know, they don't. I planted a bug in Vinton's houseboat, too. But I've never picked up so much as a peep there."

"You run across any information that might indicate where Jill Balfe is?"

He shakes his head. "Just the fact she's disappeared, too, and she and Vinton knew one another. In the bugging I've done this morning, everybody I've heard mention her seems baffled about what's happened to her, or they're putting on a good act. Of course, I have my own theory about her and Vinton, too."

"Yeah, what?"

"I don't mean a theory about where they are," Flescher says. "I mean I have a theory there's a key to what happened to both of them." He pauses and then adds softly, "I think it's that health spa in the building. He worked there, she used to go there, so did both of those other girls, and I got my suspicions it's not on the up-and-up."

"What are you driving at?"

"It's just"—he hesitates briefly—"uh, I got my doubts it's legit. I suspect the place is a front for something else.

What, I don't know, and I got nothing specific to go on. But since I've been hanging around, I've noticed a lot of traffic in and out of there at strange hours. That's why I've been concentrating so much on that building and the apartment of those girls. Sooner or later I expect to pick up a lead."

He finishes off the last of his food and lays his knife and fork down. "Good meal. You want coffee?"

"Uh-huh."

He signals the waiter for two coffees, then roots around in his coat pocket and takes out another cigarette and lights it. "What first got me wondering about that spa place is there's a guy hangs around there that's strictly bad news. I think he runs errands, does odd jobs there. He's a punk. Name's Benny Orkin—"

"Yeah, Flescher. I know him. From my days on the force. You're right; he is a punk."

Flescher nods. "He's done time. And from what I hear, he's a police informer, too, when it suits his purposes."

"That's the guy. I used to use him myself sometimes."

"Then you see what I mean. Seems an unlikely type to be working around a place like that."

The waiter brings two coffees, and Flescher asks him to leave the check.

"In addition to Benny Orkin," Flescher says, "there's the manager himself. Gregory Janish. Him and I had a talk when I first started looking for Duane Vinton. I got nothing out of him—except bad vibes. A slick article, to look at. A weight-lifter type with a black wavy pompadour—must sleep with a hairnet on to keep it just so—and he wears love beads, for God's sake. Looks like he ought to have a record—know what I mean—but I checked and he doesn't."

"About this theory of yours; let's hear it."

"Well, see, what I figure is if I'm right and there's some funny business going on in that place, either Vinton and maybe this Jill Balfe were a part of it or found out something they shouldn't have—whichever—and that accounts for why they're missing, on their own or otherwise."

"I don't know. You could be right. There's sure one thing about this case."

"What's that?"

"There are a hell of a lot of theories floating around, and few facts."

Flescher seems disappointed. "Then I'll tell you this, Spanner: I'm busting into that place, soon as the time is right, and plant me a bug. Once I do, I bet you we find I'm right." He slumps back in the chair. His eyes are blinking and his face is gray with fatigue. "Want anything else?" he asks. "Like I said, I'm picking up the check."

"Nothing else. Thanks for the dinner. I'll catch the next one."

He nods, takes out his wallet, and lays some bills on the table. Then he leans down and fumbles around the floor; he's taken his shoes off, and now he's putting them on again.

"We got a deal now, huh?" he asks. "About exchanging information?"

"Right. It's a deal, at least for the moment."

Flescher stands and picks his coat up from the back of the chair. On the way out of the restaurant, he says, "From what I overheard in that apartment today, I'd say one of those chicks—that Bobbie Gillian—goes for you. I could hear it in her voice. You could score with her, you know?" He winks.

The rain has stopped but it hasn't done much to cool off the night. Wisps of tepid smog drift in the streets and there's a moist, funky smell off the river.

Flescher is silent on the walk to where the T-Bird is parked and then, standing next to the car, he says, "You probably can't understand how much it would mean to me to find Duane Vinton. That's why I was hoping we could cooperate."

He puts a hand up and rubs his forehead. "Something I

have to tell you, Spanner. You know my agency, Trans-America Security? Well, I'm it. I mean I'm the full staff." He shakes his head. "Would you believe at one time I had two hundred and four people on the payroll, including a hundred and fifty uniformed guards? Of course, that was thirty years ago, right after I came to New York from California—"

"You worked as an investigator in California back then?"

Flescher nods.

"You ever run into a guy out there around that time named Marlowe—Philip Marlowe?"

"Marlowe—Marlowe—the name's familiar but I can't place him."

"How about a private eye named Spade, Sam Spade?"

He thinks and then shakes his head. "No."

"They were both private investigators out there. Marlowe operated around L.A., and Spade worked in San Francisco. A couple of straight guys from all I've heard. They did a lot for the business."

"I didn't work L.A. or Frisco," Flescher says. "I was located in San Diego."

"It's not important. So, you were saying about your business?"

"Oh, yeah. It's just that sometimes I can't figure out what happened. I mean, I had it made with my agency. And then, I don't know, things began to slide. Maybe it was just a matter of getting older, my attention wandering, the reflexes slowing down. It was a gradual thing, losing some business every so often, having to cut the payroll year by year, until there was only me."

Flescher pauses and looks around the street. "So here it is today, and in the state of New York there are one thousand licensed private detective agencies in business, one hundred and fifty of them listed in the Manhattan phone book Yellow Pages. And I'm one man, over sixty, wondering if I can still cut the mustard, and not a dime in savings to my name. And now a chance comes my way to pocket a fat fee if I can only put the finger on this sonofabitch Vinton. I just wanted you to know. That's why I been pushing so hard." He wipes a hand over his face. "Listen, keep in touch, will you?"

"Sure thing, Flescher. And you—hang in there."

Flescher nods and turns and trudges on down the street toward his car. As soon as he passes through the pool of murky light cast by the lamppost in the middle of the block, with his head hunched down inside the turned-up collar of his black raincoat, his figure merges with the darkness of the night as if he's vanished into thin air along with Jill Balfe and Duane Vinton.

Start thinking fanciful like that and you know it's time to head home, to a hot shower, a nightcap of a couple of slugs of Jack Daniel's, and sack out early. And then the car phone buzzes. It's Lee, the second ex-Mrs. J. T. Spanner. Her voice is a sensual whisper. "I was hoping you'd call and come by, J. T."

"I've been out on the new case that came in this morning—the missing airline stewardess. Didn't Ellie tell you about it?"

"She told me. But if you're in the car now, where are you headed?"

"Home, honey. I'm beat."

"But I want to see you," she says softly. "I've been thinking about it all day. You know."

"Baby, baby, I'm beat, bushed, out on my feet—"

"Just for a little while," she says, her voice coaxing. "It'll relax you. You want me to tell you how?"

This is an old trick of Lee's when she's in a seductive mood; to call on the car telephone, knowing perfectly well that some ham-radio or CB operator could be tuned in on the same wavelength and overhear everything that's said.

"Lee—"

"After all," she adds gently, "you were with Ellie the other night, I heard. Now I want to—see you. Fair's fair."

"All right, honey, all right. You win. I'm on my way. I'll be there in a few minutes. But I can't stay all night. And Lee, do you girls have to tell each other *everything?*"

"Everything? No. Only what you might call tit for tat." Her laugh is soft as she hangs up.

> From the Police Blotter:
> One out of three murder victims in Manhattan last year were total strangers to their killers, according to a homicide report just completed by the Police Department . . .
>
> ——*The New York Times*

THERE are two cops in plainclothes, and they stand politely in the hall after having rapped sharply on the door. They're both holding up their I.D. cards and shields. They're from the 16th Precinct. The black one—tall, slim, in his early thirties—is Sergeant Royston. His partner, around the same age and height, but ten pounds or so heavier, making his weight around 185, with blond hair and a blond brush mustache, is Sergeant Haas. Together, in their button-down shirts, rep-stripe ties, and suits with natural shoulders and two-button jackets, they make a nifty biracial advertisement for the Ivy League look.

Sergeant Royston nods in a friendly manner and asks, "You J. T. Spanner?"

"I'm Spanner. What can I do for you?"

"I believe you're acquainted with a Harry Klinger Flescher. A private investigator?"

"I know a Harry Flescher, yeah. What's this all about? I only met him last night—"

"I see," Sergeant Royston says, nodding. "Well, it's like this: Captain Tynan of the One-Six Precinct would like to talk to you. You mind coming with us?"

"You wouldn't want to tell me what it's about?"

"The captain'll tell you." Sergeant Royston smiles guilelessly as if M&M candies wouldn't melt in his mouth. "You know how it is. You mind?"

"No, it's okay. I was just finishing breakfast. Let me grab a coat and tie. You guys want to come in? You're welcome to some instant coffee."

They both look in through the open door without much interest. The apartment's just one room with a bath and a walk-in kitchen. Now the convertible sofa's pulled out, the bedclothes are still on it, and there are dirty breakfast dishes on the table by the window along with scattered sections of the morning's *New York Times*.

"We'll just wait here," Sergeant Royston says. "Thanks."

Whatever it is with Flescher, it sounds like he's somehow managed to get his ass in a sling with the law since last night. But there's no point in spending time in useless speculation; whatever it is, the cops are giving away nothing this morning. Just put on a tie and jacket, turn off the window air conditioner, and lock up the apartment.

Five minutes later, after the door's triple-locked, Sergeant Royston, waiting in the hall, says, "Really appreciate your cooperation," and presses the elevator button.

Nobody says anything else on the ride down from the third floor in the self-service elevator and on the walk across the small lobby to the street.

This morning there's a bright sun shining and the sky is pale blue and clear except for a few cottony shreds of cirrus clouds high up on the horizon to the west. The humidity is low and the air is dry and still cool, with the temperature around 70°.

The unmarked police car, a dark blue Ford Fairlane, the previous year's model, is parked in front of the building.

The two detectives sit in front. Sergeant Haas drives, accelerating fast away from the curb down 68th Street, which is one-way eastbound. The traffic light is green at Lexington Avenue, but Haas doesn't turn south, which he should have, since the 16th Precinct is over on the West Side and you'd expect him to have turned south for a block on Lexington and then west on 67th. He drives straight across, still heading east on 68th and over to Third Avenue and then Second. At Second Avenue, he turns south.

"Uh—we're not heading for the One-six Precinct, huh?"

Sergeant Royston lights a small cigar, then turns in the front seat and says, "The captain's not at the precinct right now."

"Uh-huh, I see."

Traffic is heavy on Second Avenue, even this early in the morning because the Queensboro Bridge at 59th and Second is feeding vehicles into the city from across the East River.

"Traffic generator" is the term used by the N.Y.P.D. to describe key intersections, such as the Queensboro Bridge, which are vital locations used to funnel traffic into the city—and in the hours from 7 A.M. to 10 A.M., 2,000,000 people enter the city by automobile, taxi, bus, and truck in the area between the lower tip of Manhattan and 60th Street.

Sergeant Haas opens up with the siren, clearing cars out of the way. At 42nd Street and Second Avenue, the digital time-weather clock on the *Daily News* Building reads: 7:45 . . . 71 . . . 22c . . .

Three blocks farther on, Sergeant Haas cuts off the siren and then at the next block—38th Street—swings east.

He drives on to First Avenue. In the block beyond—the block where Jill Balfe lived at Number 600—the street is jammed with police cars, two ambulances, and a police emergency van. There are uniformed police milling around on the sidewalk in front of the building with the zebra-striped canopy. Sergeant Haas leaves the car double-parked in the street after he kills the motor.

The two detectives get out. Sergeant Royston opens the rear car door and says: "Okay, Mr. Spanner, let's go."

They lead the way, on past the entrance to the apartment building and to the doorway of the Good Health Spa at the east end of the building. Two uniformed patrolmen on duty outside the spa nod at Royston and Haas and open the door.

Inside, in the spa's reception room, Sergeant Royston says: "Hope you don't mind waiting here a minute, Mr. Spanner." He disappears through double doors at the rear of the room. Sergeant Haas stays behind, wandering over to a desk where another plainclothesman, with his shield pinned to the front of his jacket, is talking on the phone and scribbling on a sheet of paper.

The reception room is longer than it is wide, and they've done it up fancy with blue carpeting, some kind of hemp fabric of matching blue covering the walls, Danish modern furniture, a grouping of armchairs and a sofa, the cushions upholstered in blue Haitian cotton, and low, white pedestal tables on which are piled an assortment of beauty and health magazines. The desk and chair back by the rear double doors—where the receptionist probably normally sits—are also Danish design. The lighting is subdued and comes from recessed fixtures in the ceiling. From somewhere—most likely the back of the spa—a smell of chlorine has seeped into the room.

Some time passes. Now and then policemen, some in uniform, some in plainclothes, move through the room from the front door to the area beyond the rear double doors and back out again. After a while a man pushes through the double doors, comes over, and nods. "J. T. Spanner? I'm Captain John Tynan."

Tynan is almost six feet tall, weighs from 170 to 175 firm pounds, has sandy hair and gray eyes, and is about forty years old. He's wearing a gray cord suit, an oxford blue shirt, a tie with red, blue, and gray stripes, and well-shined black scotch-grain shoes.

He doesn't offer his hand but he takes out a pack of Kents, shakes a couple of cigarettes loose, and says, "Have a smoke."

After he lights both cigarettes, he says, "I know you were with the department at one time, Spanner, and I've heard from Inspector Max Kauffman that in the years since you've been cooperative with us. I hope you'll be today."

"I expect to, captain. It would help if I had some idea of what this is all about."

"You know Harry Flescher—you two been working together?"

"I only met him for the first time last night. We ate dinner at a restaurant called Billy's on First Avenue. I was with him for maybe two hours altogether, from around seven to nine P.M. No, we aren't working together."

Tynan considers for a moment, then nods. "Okay, come on."

He turns and walks in long, rapid strides back through the double doors at the rear of the reception room.

The doors open into an enormous area brightly lit by the sun pouring in from windows high up on the east wall. The area runs to the back of the building. The floor is concrete and there are rows of metal clothes lockers standing against the wall in which the double doors are set. The smell of chlorine is very strong here. To the left of the doors is an olympic-size swimming pool, the sun shimmering on the water's surface. Opposite the swimming pool, to the right of the doors, are a steam room, an exercise room, a massage room. At the very back of the spa, there's a glass-enclosed office next to a door with a sign over it: EXIT. There are cops all over the place. A rubber sheet has been spread over the concrete near the edge of the pool. There's a body lying on the rubber sheet.

"Over here," Tynan says, walking ahead. At the edge of the pool, he stops and stands looking down at the body stretched out on the rubber sheet.

Harry Flescher's still wearing the blue suit he had on the night before. Now it's soaking wet and shapeless. So are his shirt and tie and shoes and socks. His left shoe lace has come untied. His right eye is closed. The cornea of his left eye has hemorrhaged, and the blood-filled socket stares sightlessly out through the open eyelids. His skin has turned a dark purple, and his face and body are ballooned up as if somebody had pumped him full of air.

"We fished him out of the pool a couple of hours ago," Tynan says. "The Puerto Rican handyman who works for the spa comes on duty about six A.M. He spotted the body in the water and called us."

"How'd he get in the pool?"

Tynan makes a flip-flop motion with his hand. "You can't see it from the way he's lying now, but he's got a hell of a gash in the back of his skull where it came into contact with something. There's a smear of blood over on the side of the pool. The M.E. set a probable estimate of the time of death as being six to eight hours ago. The M.E. also says the blow on the skull is consistent with the fact that he could have accidentally stepped off into the pool in the darkness and cracked the back of his head on the edge of the concrete. We'll have to wait for the autopsy for anything more—if there is."

"And even if somebody sapped him and dumped him in there to drown, you might never be able to prove it, huh?"

Tynan looks up alertly. "What makes you ask a question like that?"

"Before I answer, you mind telling me how you know I knew Flescher? I'm curious."

"When we found his body, we found his papers on him," Tynan says. "From his driver's license, we located his car parked outside. There was a notebook in the glove compartment in which he'd jotted down things. Your name was the last item he'd recorded in the notebook. As quickly as possible, we're trying to question everybody we can find who had any connection with him. Now, what do you know that makes you suspicious about his death?"

"It was something he said last night. You see, I'm working on a case. I think you know about it: Jill Balfe, the airline stewardess who disappeared."

Tynan nods.

"Well, what Flescher wanted to talk to me about was that he said he was working on a case, too, and he thought it might have a connection with mine."

"And what case was that?"

"Flescher said he'd been hired to look for Duane Vinton, the guy who dropped out of sight, too. As you probably know, Jill Balfe and Duane Vinton knew one another. And Vinton worked here at the spa."

Tynan frowns. "Who hired Flescher to look for Vinton? He tell you that?"

"No, he wouldn't say. He told me he'd have to check it out with his client first. He did say his client claimed Vinton had reneged on some kind of business deal before he disappeared."

"So exactly what was it Flescher said that makes you suspicious about his death?"

"He was hyped on the subject of this spa. He had some kind of theory that Jill Balfe's disappearance and Duane Vinton's were connected with the place. He told me he didn't have anything specific, but he didn't think the place was on the up-and-up. He claimed there was a guy worked around here—Benny Orkin—who had a record and was bad news. Flescher also thought there was something fishy about the manager, Janish. Apparently, Flescher'd been keeping the place under surveillance for a while, and he said there were a lot of strange comings and goings around here at odd hours."

"He tell you anything else?"

"No. Nothing important I can think of."

Tynan shakes his head wearily. "No matter what the medical facts show, Flescher died from a terminal case of stupidness. Would you believe the crazy bastard broke in here sometime last night? We found a bag he brought in with him. It was full of tools. He picked the lock to the back door. The bag also contained electronics gear. He must have been going to plant a bug in here." Very casually, he asks, "Of course, you wouldn't have known anything about what he planned to do?"

"That's breaking the law on two counts. Why would he tell me about it?"

"Yeah, sure," Tynan says, and lets it ride. Which means Flescher must have cleared the recorder and other tapes out of his car before he came back to the spa last night; otherwise, Tynan would know about the bug in the apartment where Bobbie Gillian and Karen Rushler live.

Tynan looks down at Flescher's body and then looks up again. "I don't know about his theory, but we'll keep it in mind. The inspector's back in the office there right now questioning Janish. And a couple of my men are going over things with Benny Orkin down there at the end of the pool." He points to where two plainclothesmen have Benny Orkin backed up against the wall, interrogating him.

Orkin is obviously unhappy. He's a man of about medium height, thin, in his late thirties. He has sparse reddish hair, a narrow face with small close-set eyes, and is wearing a checkered green sports coat and light-colored twill slacks. Standing facing the two plainclothesmen, he has a habit of swiveling his head from side to side every few minutes, as if he's constantly casing the area around him.

Tynan starts to say something but the detective who's been on the phone at the desk in the reception room comes over to him and interrupts. "Captain, that name we found in Flescher's papers to notify in case of accident or emergency—you know, Albert Croft, over in Fort Lee, New Jersey—"

"What about him?" Tynan asks.

"It turns out he's Flescher's lawyer," the detective says. "He says it'll take him a half hour to get into the city. I told him we'd like access to Flescher's office. He said his own office was in the same building as Flescher's, and he'd meet us there and let us in."

"All right," Tynan says. The detective walks away and Tynan says: "Look, Spanner, I'll get one of the squad cars to take you wherever—"

"Excuse me, captain. Can I ask you a favor?"

"What's that?"

"I'd like to go along when you visit Flescher's office. If there are no objections. You might find something there that'll help give me a break on the Jill Balfe case. A favor for a favor?"

Tynan thinks about it for a moment. "I don't know. Let me check."

He goes back to the glass-enclosed office at the rear of the spa. He and Inspector Kauffman stand in there, talking. The other guy—Janish—is over on the opposite side of the office from them. Then Tynan comes back. "All right, Spanner, you can go with us. The inspector says we owe you a couple of favors. We'll be leaving in fifteen or twenty minutes."

"Thanks, captain. I want to call my office while I'm waiting."

There's a pay phone over on the wall next to the row of metal clothes lockers.

Thank God, Lee is in the office early this morning. She answers the phone and says, "Where are you, J. T.? I've been calling your apartment and the car and got no answer."

"I'm working on the Jill Balfe case. Why, what's up?"

"I've only been here about ten minutes and some girl's

called you twice in that time. She sounded shook and she says it's urgent that you get in touch with her as soon as possible. Her name is Barbara Gillian—"

"What's her number, Lee?"

"It's nine-three-six-one-six-one-six."

"I'll call her. Anything else?"

"No," Lee says. "Ellie told me about the case."

"Listen, I'll be tied up for a couple of hours, I'd guess. There's something I want done. Do you have a pencil and paper?"

"Yes. Go ahead, J. T."

"There are three people I want you to get in touch with for me. One is a pilot with U.S.-Global Airlines—a Joseph Shanley—S–H–A–N–L–E–Y. If you can't find him in the phone book, try to reach him through U.S.-Global. Got it?"

"I have it, J. T."

"Then there are two stewardesses with Pan Am, Lillian Holm—H–O–L–M and Jennifer Kupperton—K–U–P–P–E–R–T–O–N. Tell the three of them who I am, that I'm working on the Jill Balfe case, and I'd like to talk to them. As you contact them, space out the appointments starting this afternoon, if possible."

"I understand," Lee says.

"I'll call Barbara Gillian now. I should be in the office within a couple of hours or I'll check with you. Okay, honey?"

"Okay. Bye-bye, J. T."

On the next phone call, Bobbie Gillian answers on the first ring. Her voice sounds breathless. "H-H-Hello?"

"This is J. T. Spanner."

Her next words come in a rush. "I thought you'd want to know. There's something going on downstairs here at my building, in that health spa. I can't find out what it is but there are police everywhere around the place—"

"Yes, I know about it, Miss Gillian. I'm in the spa right now. That's where I'm calling you from."

"You *are?*" she asks, surprised. "I—I—thought—I don't know—that maybe it had something to do with Jill or Duane Vinton—you mentioned the spa yesterday—and you'd want to know."

"I don't have all the facts yet, but there's nothing to indicate that this is connected with them. I'll tell you more when I know more."

"I don't know exactly why, but seeing all the police in front of the building spooked me," Bobbie Gillian says. "I guess it's because I'm alone—Karen went out on a flight this morning."

"I don't think there's any reason for you to be upset, Miss Gillian. But I'll tell you what—if you'd like, I'll check with you a little later and see if you're all right."

"I don't want to be a bother but I'd like that."

"It'll be a few hours before I can call you. You take it easy now. Okay?"

"Thank you," she says softly.

A couple of guys from the city morgue have arrived now. They're carrying a canvas body bag. They go over to where Flescher's body is lying.

A small Latin-looking man, dressed in a blue shirt and blue denims, walks past; he's probably the handyman Tynan mentioned.

"Amigo, you have a minute?"

He stops and turns. "Si?"

"Can I talk to you?"

He walks over. "Oh, yes. Si."

"You're the fellow who found the body in the pool?"

He nods. "Is bad, yes?" He probably thinks he's talking to one of the plainclothesmen assigned to the investigation. He's about twenty-five years old and underweight even for his 5'6" height. His skin is a dusky olive shade, and he has black hair and large, sad black eyes.

"Have you been working here at the spa long?"

"From the first?"

"Yes, from the first. How long?"

"Maybe almost two years."

"The other fellow who used to work here up until last week—Vinton, Duane Vinton. You know, did you know him?"

"Vinton. Si," he says.

"Tell me about him. What kind of man was he?"

He shrugs. He thinks for a moment. *"Brageta Brava,"* he says emphatically.

"What does that mean—*'Brageta Brava'?*"

"Means 'pants fly'—a lady chaser—and catches them, too."

"Has he been around at all since he last worked here? Have you seen him?"

The handyman shakes his head but now his attention is distracted. He's looking over toward the edge of the pool where the two morgue guys have lifted up Harry Flescher's corpse and are putting it into the canvas body bag. Everyone else in the place is watching, too. Inspector Max Kauffman has come out of the office at the far end of the area and is standing, hands clasped behind his back, observing the scene. Gregory Janish, the manager of the spa, has also come out of the office and is watching. Flescher's description of Janish last night was accurate enough to make the man recognizable today. Square. Muscular. A rolling pompadour of thick black hair. Swarthy complexion. Ass-hugging chinos. Open-neck shirt with a chain of love beads showing against his hairy chest.

It's silent in the spa now. The two men from the morgue strap the body into the bag, with the feet sticking out. Flescher's untied left shoe falls off, and one of the men picks up the shoe and stuffs it into his coat pocket. Then the two men lift the bag, one at either end and, staggering under the dead weight, carry it out through the front of the spa. The Puerto Rican handyman makes the sign of the cross and walks away, head shaking.

Inspector Max Kauffman strolls over and nods. "Spanner."

"Hello, Inspector."

Max Kauffman's in his early fifties, a powerful-looking man, broad-shouldered and barrel-chested, with the kind of stocky body that makes him appear shorter than his actual height of one inch less than six feet. There are a few streaks of gray at the temples of his wavy black hair. He is, as always, fastidiously groomed; as usual, he is wearing a Savile Row suit—this one of summer-weight gray with a hair-thin black stripe.

The inspector smoothes his right eyebrow with a finger. "Captain Tynan's reported to me your account of your conversation with Harry Flescher last night."

"Yes, sir."

"It's probably not going to help us any, but still it's useful for the department to have such information." That's as close as Max Kauffman ever comes to paying a compliment. He always manages to position himself at an emotional distance—most of the men under his command never get close enough to form an opinion of him at all; the others who do don't always like him, except for maybe one or two, but they all respect him.

"Yes, sir."

"I understand you're working on that missing-persons case and that you'd like to be at Flescher's office when we examine it. I've agreed you can accompany us."

He pauses before he says, "But—Spanner—I want there to be no mistake about one thing: even if there's a connection between what Flescher was working on and your case, or between his death and your case, from here on in, whatever you find, you tell *us*. No playing cop on your own. You saw what happened to Flescher. Do you read me?"

"I read you."

Max Kauffman nods and walks away.

Tynan, who's been standing at a distance while the inspector was talking, now comes over.

"Let's go, Spanner."

"That inspector of yours, captain—"

"Yeah?"

"I think he wanted to say something nice to me, but I guess he got all choked up and the words just wouldn't come out."

Tynan isn't amused. "Don't press your luck, Spanner," he says tightly.

Cops.

> . . . According to some sources, the first
> wiretapping ever took place right here in
> Manhattan, back in 1895. Wiretappers in
> those days cut the insulation from tele-
> phone lines and clamped wires leading to
> headsets onto the exposed telephone lines,
> listened, and took notes of conversations . . .

HARRY Flescher's office is on the third floor of a grimy sandstone building on West 42nd Street. It's the kind of building where the names on the directory listing in the tiny lobby all sound like fakes—U-Buy-It Tie Co., Busy-As-A-B Employment Agency, The Odd Notions Corp., The P-D-Q Speedwriting School, and more of the same—and the elevator's one of those outdated models that creaks and clanks and wheezes and sways as it creeps upwards and is large enough to accommodate a truckload of freight. Today, it's accommodating nine plainclothes detectives, one police captain, one deputy chief inspector, one private eye, and one little old lady in a gingham dress down to just above her ankles and, below that, white socks and open-toed wedgies, and is lugging a stuffed shopping bag in either hand—and wouldn't it be a gas if she's one of the city's corps of little-old-lady shoplifters. She gets off at the second floor.

Up on the third floor there's a man in a dark suit pacing

the hall in front of an office door on which is printed in tarnished gold-colored letters: TransAmerica SECURITY AGENCY.

Tynan is the first one off the elevator. He introduces himself to the dark-suited man who, in turn, says his name is Albert Croft.

Croft takes a bunch of keys on a silver ring out of his pocket and uses one of the keys to open the door. He flips a light switch inside the office and everybody troops in.

The room inside is approximately 12 x 12, and the figured green rug on the floor is smaller by approximately two inches square. Closed venetian blinds cover the one window at the far end of the room. In front of the window, facing the door, is a walnut pedestal desk with a high-backed swivel chair behind it; and in front of the desk there are three armchairs arranged in a semicircle with their backs to the door. There are a dozen six-drawer green metal file cabinets against one wall and a glass-front walnut bookcase against the other wall. On the far side of the bookcase is a closed door. The air is hot and hazy with dust, and there's a coating of dust on the venetian blinds, the desk, the chairs, the filing cabinets, and the bookcase, outside and in, where it is impossible to read through the glass front the titles of the dusty book jackets lining the shelves.

Tynan stands in the center of the room, gazes around, and says to the detectives, "Okay, start searching through everything here. I want to particularly see anything that has the name Duane Vinton on it, or Jill Balfe, Gregory Janish, Benny Orkin, or The Good Health Spa."

The men start emptying out the file cabinets, the desk, and the bookcase, which creates more dust in the room.

Inspector Kauffman has taken a cigar out of his pocket. He puts it in his mouth but doesn't light it while he glances around.

Albert Croft, the lawyer, is patting his perspiring face with a handkerchief. He's in his sixties, on the slim side, medium height, with a shaggy mane of white hair, a narrow head and face. He has thin, bloodless lips, not much of a chin, white eyebrows that need a barber's scissors, and is wearing rimless eyeglasses with gold earpieces. His suit is black silk, and with it he has on a white-on-white shirt with onyx cuff links, a silver tie, and straight-tip black shoes that need a shine.

The inspector walks over to the closed door in the rear of the office and opens it. You can see that the space in there is not much more than a cubbyhole. The light comes from a dingy window above a washbasin and toilet. Crowded into the rest of the cubbyhole is a rollaway cot, opened up, which has rumpled sheets and a pillow on it, a small table with a hot plate on top, and a two-drawer file cabinet. Two suits—one brown, one gray—are hanging on coat hangers from a couple of nails in the wall at the foot of the cot. Inspector Kauffman opens the drawers of the file cabinet. There are more shirts in there, some socks, and underwear.

"The poor sonofabitch must have been living here," the inspector says.

Croft makes a meaningless gesture with his hands. "I knew he'd been down on his luck, but not that far down."

Inspector Kauffman closes the door. He paces the floor of the outer office impatiently. Now there are papers, file folders, and books strewn all over the place. Tynan has led Albert Croft over by the window and is questioning him in a low voice, probably about what the lawyer knew of Flescher's activities before his death. It looks as if he's getting nowhere since Croft keeps shaking his head.

From the way the piles of papers are accumulating on the floor as the detectives go through the file cabinets and desk, Flescher must have been a guy who threw away almost nothing. Finally, after a while, one of the detectives calls out, "Captain, I think I found something."

Tynan goes over to the man, and Max Kauffman follows. The three of them stand close together, talking, looking at an open file folder. Then Tynan closes the file and sticks it under his arm. Max Kauffman starts prowling restlessly around the office again. Tynan comes across the room.

"Anything, captain?"

"Not much, Spanner," he says distractedly. "The lawyer claims he doesn't know anything about Flescher's investigative work. We found a file Flescher had on Vinton, but there's nothing in there that you and I didn't already know, no clue to who hired him to look for Vinton. About the only new item in there was a dozen prints of a photograph of Vinton."

"Would it be possible for me to have one of those photographs?"

"I guess so," Tynan says. He takes one of the photographs out and hands it over and walks away.

The glossy print is a black and white head-and-chest shot of Duane Vinton. He's wearing a sporty-looking cashmere jacket with lapels that flare out beyond the frames of the photograph and an open-collar shirt with a fluffed-up ascot inside. He's thirty-something and has broad shoulders and a craggy kind of face with a large nose and high cheekbones. He has sideburns down to his earlobes and darkish blond hair which he's combing, head cocked to one side, while looking into the camera as if it were a mirror.

Time passes slowly for the next half hour while the police continue to search through Flescher's papers and books until finally Tynan calls a halt.

"I'm going to put a padlock on the door," Tynan tells Albert Croft. "Unless you have any objections?" The lawyer shrugs.

A couple of detectives remain behind in the office until Tynan can send a locksmith back from the precinct.

Out in the hall, Albert Croft mops his face some more with his handkerchief, then takes an elevator to a higher floor. Everybody else rides another elevator to the lobby.

Walking out to the street, Tynan asks, "Drop you someplace, Spanner?"

"No thanks. I'm going to grab a cab to my office."

Tynan, Max Kauffman, and the other policemen climb into the waiting squad cars and leave.

Back in the lobby, the directory listing for Albert Croft's office is the sixth floor. This time there's nobody else in the elevator.

Croft's name is on the door of an office next to the building's inside stairwell. The door is unlocked and inside is a small anteroom. The walls of the anteroom are a bilious green with dark wood wainscoting running halfway up the walls. There's a green carpet on the floor. There's a row of chairs for waiting clients—today there are no clients waiting—and there's a small desk and typewriter. There's a bony-faced gray-haired woman in her fifties sitting at the desk. There's an inner door—closed—at the back of the anteroom.

The woman looks up. "Yes, sir?" Her voice is high, nasal. "May I help—Sir!" She's quite agitated now. "You can't go in there!" She's on her feet, jabbering away.

The inner door opens into an office about the size of Harry Flescher's office three floors below. The color scheme—green walls with dark wood wainscoting and green carpeting—is the same as in the anteroom. There are some bookcases around three of the walls, the fourth wall has windows in it and a window air conditioner, and there's a large desk set catercorner in the middle of the room. Albert Croft is sitting in a leather chair with his feet crossed, propped up on the desk. On the desk, too, are about a dozen reels of tape and a tape recorder. He's listening to the tape recorder. The voice on the tape—Bobbie Gillian's voice—is saying:

". . . not hard to get along with. At first, when she moved in here with us, about three years ago, she seemed . . ."

Croft jerks his feet off the desk and stands. He quickly

87

turns the tape recorder off. His face is flushed a deep red.

"What are you doing here?" he demands. "You can't come barging—"

Back in the doorway, his secretary is screeching, "He walked right in. He wouldn't stop!"

"Shut up, Croft, and sit down. Do you know you're guilty of breaking the law, removing those tape recordings from Flescher's office?"

"Where's your warrant?" he asks. "You can't come—"

"I'm not a cop, Croft. But if you don't do what I tell you to do, I'm going to call the cops. They'll bring a warrant all right when they come. Now, do what I tell you to do. Shut up and sit down. And tell her to shut up, too, and get back to her desk and shut the door behind her. Do it."

"Listen," Croft says frantically, "I—"

"I told you what I want you to do, Croft. And I want you to do it, *now!*"

Croft gulps a couple of times and nods his head. "All right, Naomi," he says in a choked voice, "go back to your desk and keep quiet. And close the door."

She goes out, shutting the door behind her.

Croft sits down in his chair and mops his face and head with a handkerchief. "If you're not a cop, what were you doing down in Flescher's office? What's this all about?"

"What this is all about is I'm going to protect you from going to jail for concealing evidence and obstructing justice, in the matter of those tape recordings. What I have in mind, Croft, is that you and I are going to enter into a limited partnership."

"What're you talking about? You crazy? What partnership? I'm not saying anything else until I know who you are."

"I'm a private investigator, like Harry Flescher was. My name is J. T. Spanner. You just heard it and my voice on those tapes you were listening to. As you just heard on those tapes I'm investigating the disappearance of a girl named Jill Balfe."

Croft's regained some of his composure. "What's all that got to do with me?"

"We'll discuss that in a moment. But first I want you to know that last night Harry Flescher and I had a long talk. He tailed me after he taped that conversation you were just listening to. He told me all about the bugging he'd been doing. But the police don't know about it. Yet. So while I was there when the police searched his office and there were no tapes, I figured you'd removed them before we got there. It looks like I was right."

Croft pats his face and head with his handkerchief; he's not sweating as much now. "I still want to know what all that's got to do with me?"

"Most of it doesn't have anything to do with you, as far as I know. The tapes do. Like I said, you're guilty of concealing evidence, et cetera. You need a partner—me—to see that you don't go to jail."

Croft's eyes narrow. "And exactly what do you get out of this partnership? Money? Blackmail, is that it?"

"Ah, no, Croft. I'm not interested in money. Not your money, anyway. It is curious, though, that you should mention blackmail. I would imagine that might be one of the motives the police would come up with to account for your removing the tapes."

Croft's sweating harder again. He starts to say something, but instead just wipes his face and head.

"Anyhow, Croft, actually what I had in mind was that insofar as these tapes are concerned, we make an agreement: I become your private investigator and you become my lawyer. Only in this one instance."

"I don't get it," Croft says. "What's that going to accomplish?"

"Client confidentiality, of course. Legally, or quasi-legally, I could withhold giving information about you, and vice versa. You see?"

"And that's all there is to it?"

"That's all. Ah—except, naturally, I'd take the tapes with me."

Croft doesn't say anything.

"I'm sure you can appreciate the reasonableness of that. After all, I'm legitimately employed on a case, and those tapes might have a bearing on my case. Until I determine that fact, I'd have an obligation to my client not to turn the tapes over to the police."

Croft still doesn't say anything.

"Or, let's look at it from your angle, Croft. If you don't have the tapes on your hands, it'll be a lot easier on you. You won't have to worry. Like, for example, that the cops might pop in here the minute I leave."

Croft leans back in his chair. "All right," he says softly, "I get the point."

"Good. Good. We've got a deal? Let's shake on it."

Croft's hand is slick with sweat, but he manages a strained smile. There's a cardboard box on the floor by the desk. He puts the box on the desk, unplugs the tape recorder, and begins packing the recorder and the tapes in the box.

"Listen," Croft says, "I want you to know I wasn't thinking about blackmail. I took the recorder and tapes out of Harry's office on impulse. Then my curiosity was too great not to listen to them."

"You don't have to convince me of anything, Croft. All I'm interested in is what happened to that missing girl I'm looking for. It may be that the tapes'll help. No hard feelings, huh?"

Croft shakes his head slowly.

"Then I'll be on my way."

The box is bulky to carry but not too heavy. Croft goes ahead through the anteroom and opens the door to the hall. His secretary is sitting at her desk. She gives a disapproving sniff in farewell.

Croft stands in the doorway until the elevator comes. As

the elevator doors close, the last sight of him is with his handkerchief out again, wiping at his face. He's a real sweetheart, the type of lawyer who, give him enough rope, he'll hang his own client. Every time.

He'll probably keep quiet about the tapes but you never know. Just to be on the safe side, it might be a good idea to find a place for them where they can be transcribed away from the office. The shortest cab ride is to Ellie's apartment down on Washington Square.

Outside, the day is starting to heat up. The sky is a cloudless blue, and the sun is almost directly overhead. There's still one squad car parked in front of the office building. There are plenty of empty cabs cruising West 42nd Street. The one which pulls over is Cab No. 8Z1104, and the hack license identifies the driver as Anthony Labanni. He's in his sixties, has stubby gray hair, and is wearing an Hawaiian print sports shirt with a towel around his neck to soak up the sweat.

"Fifth Avenue and Eighth Street."

"Right on," he says. As he pulls out into traffic, he glances into the rearview mirror. "Say, young fellow, I've got one for you: what's the difference between a snow man and a snow woman?"

"Okay, tell me. What's the difference?"

"Snowballs."

And in show business, they're always asking where the new comics are going to come from, now that burlesque and vaudeville are dead.

> The Manhattan District Attorney's office announced this morning that one hundred suspected felons had been arrested as the result of a fake fencing operation set up by the Police Department. Several months ago, the D.A. said, detectives posing as fences and working out of a rented storefront on Ninth Avenue in midtown began buying up loot from alleged criminals involved in countless robberies and burglaries. Police, meanwhile, were collecting evidence which led to today's arrests ...
>
> ——*Late City Edition, the* New York Post

IT'S several minutes past 1:00 P.M. and Lee and Ellie are both in the office which is unusual since they almost always take a full noon-to-two lunch together, turning the phones over to the answering service while they're out.

Lee's busy at the typewriter, and Ellie's pacing up and down, a large white handbag slung over her shoulder.

"J. T.!" Ellie says. "Where've you been? We've been trying to reach you everywhere."

Lee stops typing and rests her arms on top of the typewriter carriage.

"I've been in transit, honey. And then I had a quick lunch. Why, what's up?"

"I was just typing up a note to leave for you," Lee says. She pulls the sheet of paper from the typewriter. "It's been busy this morning." She glances at the sheet of paper. "Sergeant Hornstein of the Sixteenth Precinct called and wants you to call him back. And those two Pan Am stewardesses you asked me to contact—Holm and

Kupperton?—they're on their way in to see you. They said they'd be here between one and one-thirty. That pilot you asked me to call for you. Joseph Shanley? He's in town and I have his home phone number, but so far I haven't been able to contact him."

Lee pauses, takes a breath, and continues. "Also, some man's been calling you approximately every half hour for the last couple of hours. He wouldn't identify himself, but he said it's urgent that he talk to you. Every time he called, he said if you called in, to ask you to leave a number where he could reach you. The last time he called, he said he'd call back in about thirty minutes, and it's been almost that now. Oh, and John Macauley and that Mrs. Margaret Balfe both called. Macauley said he was just checking to see if we'd heard from you this morning. I said I had. He said you didn't have to return his call. And Mrs. Balfe said she didn't want to bother you, but she wondered if you had any news, no matter how small, to tell her yet."

"Is that it?"

"That's it," Lee says. "We didn't want to leave without telling you."

"Thanks for waiting. Look, something's come up that I want to talk to you both about. This morning I came into possession of a tape recorder and some tapes. Confidential stuff that may possibly contain some information about Jill Balfe. I went down and stashed them in your apartment, Ellie. That's just in case the cops should come looking around here with a search warrant. Which I don't think's going to happen. But just in case. From here on, no matter what comes up, neither of you know anything about the tapes. Remember that."

They both nod.

"I need the tapes transcribed. I thought maybe the two of you could work on them there, in shifts. I'd like the transcripts done as soon as possible. Could you arrange a schedule between you?"

"We'll take care of it," Ellie says.

"Good. And figure out some kind of identification system for tapes and transcripts as you do them so if I find something in the transcript that I want to hear, I'll know which tape it's on. Oh, and listen to all the tapes from beginning to end, even when there are long periods of dead air."

They both nod.

"The tapes and recorder are in a cardboard box. I put them on the top shelf of your bedroom closet, Ellie, and covered the box with one of your robes. Let's keep them out of sight when you're not there."

"You want me to put through a call to Sergeant Hornstein?" Lee asks. "And would you like us to stick around until those stewardesses show up?"

"No, that's all right, honey. I'll take over. What I want you both to do is get out of here and get some lunch. By the way, did I happen to mention that you both look particularly fetching today?"

It's true. Ellie's wearing a powder-blue sleeveless sunback, the skirt short and straight, and white low-heel slingbacks. Lee's pale blonde hair is parted in the middle and pulled back over her ears and caught in a chignon in back. She has on a black linen halter dress, arms and back bare, and sandals with black straps.

They like the compliment and they leave smiling.

The phone rings.

"This is J. T. Spanner."

There are a couple of seconds of hum on the line before a man's voice says warily, "Spanner?"

"Yeah, yeah, this is Spanner. Who's this?"

The answer comes in a whisper. "Benny. You know. *Benny*."

"Come on, come on, for Christ's sake! Benny who?"

There's another pause and you can almost see him at the other end of the line glancing all around furtively before he whispers: "Orkin. You know."

"Oh, *that* Benny. Yeah, sure. How are you, Benny?"

"That's what I'm calling you in regards to. How I am. How I am is in a hole that's over my ass. Which might not sound like it's all that deep unless you understand I'm in this hole head-down, you understand?"

"I'd say that sounds deep, all right, Benny, yeah."

"Now the thing is," Orkin says, "I figured seeing as how we've done some favors for one another in the past, maybe I give you a call and maybe we get together and maybe we see if the old magic still works."

"From your end, it probably sounds like a reasonable proposition, all right, Benny. But the truth is, I can't think of any favors you can do for me."

"Don't be too one hundred percent certain about that. I didn't see you at the place this morning, the health club?"

"Yeah. You saw me. I saw you. So?"

"What I mean," Orkin says slowly, "is I was wondering what your interest was. You just happened by, or what?"

"I knew Harry Flescher, the guy who got it in the pool. Why, what's it to you?"

"You were working with him on a case or what? It could be if I knew your angle, maybe I could do you a favor in the way of telling you some things in exchange for you do me one, you understand?"

"I wasn't working with Flescher. He told me he'd been hired to look for Duane Vinton. I'm working on a different case. I'm looking for that airline stewardess who disappeared. Jill Balfe."

There's another long pause on the line before Benny Orkin says, "See the way it turns out? It just so happens I'm in a very good position to do you a favor on that one. So now maybe we get together after all and give the old magic a chance to do its stuff again?"

"I'm not buying bullshit, Benny."

"Who's talking bullshit?" His voice is indignant now.

"You give me one example somebody paid me for delivering bullshit and I'll kiss your ass in Macy's window. It's never happened. And I been paid plenty."

"All right, Benny. You have a point there. What did you have in mind as the size of the favor I do for you?"

"Well," he says, "I got to keep out of sight for a while. So my expenses won't run much. Maybe it's possible I can keep doing you favors while I'm out of sight. Say our first meeting you do me a favor in the neighborhood of two Cs."

"Sounds high. But we'll talk. I can see you later today. Where?"

"Lemme think." He pauses for a moment and then says: "I'll be in Room three-two-one, the Sydney Hotel, West Forty-eighth Street. That's between Broadway and Eighth Avenue. Actually, the room belongs to a friend of mine by the name of Ginger Higget. That's in case anybody should inquire at the hotel as to who you're visiting, not that that'll likely occur."

"All right, Benny, I'll see you there at five o'clock."

"Oh, and there's this other thing, Spanner."

"What's that?"

"I'm really jammed up, you understand?" he says. "I don't want nobody to know where I am, especially the cops. I mean, they're not officially looking for me or anything like that, so you don't have to worry. But there are a couple of guys, and I'm not going to say who, might be looking to fix it so I'm not in any condition to do any favors for anybody—permanently. You understand?"

"I understand, Benny. Not to worry."

"That's the stuff. A guy's got to have somebody to trust, and you never fucked me yet."

Orkin hangs up.

Along with the message to call Sergeant Hornstein, Lee has typed up the 16th Precinct phone number. The number is 7-5-2-7-6-5-5.

The switchboard answers: "Sixteenth Precinct, Officer Remley."

"I'd like to speak to Sergeant Hornstein in Missing Persons."

There are a couple of rings at the other end of the line before the phone is picked up.

"Missing Persons, Sergeant Hornstein," Hornstein says.

"Sergeant, this is J. T. Spanner. You left word for me to call?"

"Oh, yeah, Spanner," he says. "It may turn out to be nothing, but then again I thought you ought to know. On the Jill Balfe case. This morning a Con Edison crew working in Kew Gardens, Queens, came across a pretty decomposed body stuffed into one of the sewers over there."

"Any indications it might be her body?"

"Well, from what I hear, the corpse fits her as far as the size goes, and Kew Gardens isn't all that far from JFK Airport. That's about all I know about it. They've got the corpse at the M.E.'s office right now, to run tests on it and comparisons with Jill Balfe's dental charts. I find out anything else, I'll let you know."

"Thanks, sergeant."

"It's okay," Hornstein says. "Listen, Spanner, Captain Tynan gave me a fast briefing on the drowning this morning at that health spa. That Flescher guy? The captain mentioned something about he'd talked to you, that you knew Flescher or something?"

"Can you hang on a minute, sergeant?"

"I'll hold."

The door from the hall to the outer office has opened, and two girls come in.

"Ladies, you looking for me? J. T. Spanner?"

"Yes," one of them says. "We were told you wanted to see us. About Jill Balfe—"

"Yes indeed. Have a seat there for a minute, please.

I'm on the phone but I'll be right with you . . . uh, hello, sergeant?"

"I'm here, Spanner," Hornstein says. "Somebody came in. Am I right? Can you talk?"

"I'll try. To answer your question, I met that party just once—last night—and we had a talk. I frankly don't know what to make of what happened this morning."

"Let me ask you: he—Flescher—did tell you he'd been hired to look for Duane Vinton? You told the captain he'd told you that, huh?"

"That's right."

"But Flescher didn't have any information about Jill Balfe?" Hornstein asks.

"He said not."

"You think his drowning in the pool was an accident?"

"My hunch is that it wasn't."

"Tell you what," Hornstein says. "Let's see what the outcome is on that corpse that turned up this morning. Then maybe you and I can get together and compare notes."

"Okay, and thanks for keeping me up to date."

He grunts something and that ends the conversation.

The two stewardesses who have come in during the telephone conversation are sitting in the outer office, near the reception desk.

"Hello, I'm J. T. Spanner. Why don't you both come on back into my office?"

One of the girls has dark brown hair and the other is an ash blonde. When they're seated on the other side of the desk, the one with dark brown hair says, "I'm Jenny Kupperton." The other one says, "And I'm Lillian Holm."

They're both tall, slim, shapely, good-lookers. Jenny Kupperton is dressed in a light tan pantsuit with a wispy gold kerchief around her throat, and gold sandals. Lillian Holm is wearing a floral-print chintz skirt that falls below her knees, a mint-green cotton T-shirt with quarter-length sleeves, and rope-soled espadrilles that have multicolored ribbon laces which wrap around her ankles.

"I appreciate your coming to see me. As my secretary probably told you, I'm trying to find out what became of Jill Balfe. Her mother hired me for the job. I know the two of you were among the last persons to see her at the airport before she disappeared and that you've already talked to the police. I just wanted to hear—for myself—about that last time you saw her."

They look at each other. Lillian Holm makes a gesture to Jenny Kupperton and nods.

Jenny Kupperton frowns and says slowly, "I—we—Lillian and I—have thought about that night and talked about it, again and again ever since we first knew Jill had disappeared. Neither of us have been able to recall anything significant about the occurrence."

"Suppose you describe the circumstances to me. What time it was, exactly where you saw her, how she appeared."

"Lillian and I saw her separately that night," Jenny Kupperton says. "We—Lillian and I—had both worked the same run that evening, from Rome to New York. I'd left the plane before Lillian and was on the way to the Pan Am offices when I passed Jill. It must have been close to ten P.M. She was carrying her flight bag."

"You were friends, then, you'd met before?"

"She'd been to a couple of parties at our place. For a while I was dating one of the U.S.-G pilots, Joe Shanley, and he knew Jill and introduced her to us. We invited her to a couple of bashes."

"Okay, now about that night. It was close to ten P.M. and she's carrying her flight bag—"

Jenny Kupperton nods. "I assumed she was on her way to the U.S.-G Building; she was headed in that direction. We didn't stop and talk, just exchanged words in passing.

I said, 'Where you in from?' And she said, 'Belgium. How about you?' And I said, 'Rome.' And we both said something about getting together soon. And that was it.''

"What kind of mood would you say she was in?"

"Normal, cheerful, I guess," Jenny Kupperton says. "I don't know what else to tell you." She looks toward Lillian Holm. "Lillian?"

"I wasn't too far in back of Jenny when I passed Jill," Lillian Holm says. It was almost directly in front of the U.S.-G Building and I, too, assumed that's where she was going. We both said hi, and she said something about she just saw my roommate and maybe we could all get together soon. She seemed to me just like she'd always seemed the times I'd been around her before."

"And neither of you noticed anyone else around the area where she was, anyone that might have been waiting for her, or following her?"

They both shake their heads.

"Of course," Jenny Kupperton says, "there were other people around. Passengers, airport personnel, but I didn't notice anyone in particular who seemed to have a special interest in Jill."

"I didn't either," Lillian Holm says.

"Yeah. Now, to go back for a moment to those two parties you invited Jill to. Did anyone come with her? A date?"

They both shake their heads. "She came alone both times," Jenny Kupperton says. "She was just there with everybody else—a friend of Joe's, Joe Shanley, the pilot I mentioned."

"Okay. There's one more favor I'd like to ask of you. I have a photograph here. I'd like to know if you know the guy or if you've ever seen him any place before."

They lean forward over the desk and look at the photograph of Duane Vinton.

"No," Jenny Kupperton says, "I don't know him. I've never seen him before as far as I know."

Lillian Holm continues to study the photograph and doesn't say anything.

"Miss Holm?"

She looks up, an uncertain expression on her face. "I don't know him." She shakes her head. "But—but I think I've seen him before." She bites her lip. "Oh, this is weird—"

"What? What's weird?"

"Maybe it's only the power of suggestion." She taps her thumb against her forehead. "I can't swear to it, but I think I saw him out at JFK that same night." She keeps tapping her thumb against her forehead.

"Yes, go on."

"Oh, I don't know whether it's the same guy or not. Let me explain."

She pauses, thinks for a moment, and says: "What happened was after I'd checked in with the office and goofed around there for a while, I came back outside and was walking up and down, waiting for Jenny so we could come into the city together. And there was a guy walking up and down out there, too, like he was waiting for somebody."

She pinches a crease in her forehead between her thumb and finger. "This guy who was walking up and down, he glances over at me several times and then he says something like if the people we're each waiting for don't show up, maybe he and I should get together. My answer was an unladylike 'four-letter-word *you,* buster,' and he laughed and I went back inside the building to wait for Jenny. When Jenny and I came outside again, he was gone."

She pauses, looks down at the photograph again, and says: "I never thought of him since until you showed me this picture. I don't even know if it was the same guy or not. But the guy that night was wearing an ascot, too, I remember, and as well as I can recall resembled this guy in the picture. I don't know. I wish I could be more definite." Her words trail off.

"Now, when this character was walking up and down that night, how close was he to the U.S.-G Airlines Building? Do you think he could have been waiting for somebody—say, Jill Balfe—to come out of there?"

"Well, he was in sight of the building, yes," Lillian Holm says. "I suppose he could have been waiting for her—" She pauses, looks puzzled, and then asks, "Why are you shaking your head?"

"Because I just remembered that Jill Balfe never reported to the U.S.-G. office. So he couldn't have been waiting for her—unless, of course, he didn't know she wasn't in there. There's always that possibility. Hey, am I confusing you?"

"Maybe a little," she says, a hesitant smile on her face.

"Only a little? Hell, I'm confusing myself a lot."

They both laugh.

"Mr. Spanner," Jenny Kupperton says, "who is the man in the photograph? Are you at liberty to tell us?"

"His name is Duane Vinton. He and Jill dated a few times."

"You couldn't just ask him if he was at the airport that night?" Lillian Holm asks.

"He hasn't been around for a while, either."

They're both silent for a moment. Then Jenny Kupperton asks: "I suppose everybody's already thought of the possibility that they might have gone away together?"

"Yes, it's been thought of."

"Is there anything else, Mr. Spanner?" Jenny Kupperton asks.

"No. I guess that covers it. And I really do thank you for your cooperation, both of you."

They nod and get up to leave.

At the door to the hall, Lillian Holm says, "I hope you find Jill, Mr. Spanner. *Him*—if he's the same guy I saw that night—I hope stays lost."

... New York City has over 200 hotels with over 100,000 rooms to be filled each day, which accommodate 16,000,000 out-of-town visitors annually and there are over 1,000 robberies of hotel rooms each year ...

"Who is it?" Benny Orkin whispers, one eye staring out through the open crack of the door to Room 321 of the Sydney Hotel.

"Who the fuck do you think it is? You're looking straight at me."

"Right, right, Spanner," Orkin says quickly and yanks the door open. "Come on in, come on in."

Then he slams the door quickly and locks it with a key. Before he turns around, he fits a police lock into place, shoving a thick iron bar down through a steel brace bolted to the inside of the door under the knob and into a heavy metal slot attached to the floor.

The room is small. In it are a double bed, a dresser, a wooden table, and two wooden chairs. You have to turn sideways to squeeze through the space between the five pieces of furniture. The one window, on the opposite side of the room from the door to the hall, has a dark shade pulled down to an inch or so above the sill, no curtains.

There's a lamp on the table and an overhead bulb in the ceiling. They're both on, but there are still shadows in the corners. The wallpaper is washed-out pink streaked with what look like water stains near the ceiling and peeling away in strips at the baseboards. The piece of carpet on the floor is tobacco-colored. The door is open to the not-much-more-than 2x4 bathroom.

On top of the table is a paper plate with four cigarette butts floating in a quarter-inch puddle of soupy gravy, a styrofoam cup, and a half-empty fifth of something called Pó-tash Vodka. The bed is unmade and scattered across it are several copies of *The Racing Form* and eight or nine scratch sheets. The room smells of cigarette smoke and greasy food and feels like the Temperature-Humidity-Index in there ought to register a 99 reading.

Benny Orkin turns from the door and says anxiously: "You sure you didn't tell nobody about this meeting, huh, Spanner?"

"No, nobody. Relax, Benny. All you have to worry about is that you have something to trade me for that C-note you want."

"Two Cs was the figure was mentioned." Orkin holds up two fingers.

"Must have been a bad connection. Anyhow, a C-note, two Cs, first you got to sell me you've got something to sell. You know how we've always done business. And sit down. Standing up like that is bad for your hemorrhoids."

Orkin shakes his head. "Where'd you get it I got piles?"

"That pained expression on your face. I figured that's what it had to be."

Orkin comes over to the table and sits down in the other chair. He's still wearing the light-colored twill slacks he had on this morning, but now he's in his undershirt and stocking feet. He runs a hand nervously through his reddish hair, a worried look on his face. "Listen," he says seriously, "when I told you on the phone I had some stuff

I could tell you might help this particular case of yours, I figured you'd figure it was worth two Cs."

"*Talk,* for Christ's sake!"

Orkin swivels his head, glancing right and left as he says, "Now, I don't know nothing directly about what happened to this broad, you understand? But I know her from she was hanging around the place, the spa. She was I think stuck on this person Duane Vinton you also mentioned on the phone."

"Yeah, I know all about that, Benny, and—that—Vinton—has—disappeared—too. So what's new?"

Orkin nods. "What's new is suppose I could hand you some information that might could tie him—Vinton—into that body they think was hers that was stolen, how much would that be worth?"

"'Might could tie him in,' that sounds like pretty iffy information, Benny."

"Hell, I'd say it could be, you understand, like prima facie, depending upon how you look at it."

"Benny, Benny, Benny, prima facie means something *is* true the first time you look at it, *you understand?*"

"Yeah," he says, "well, that's what I think this information is, anyhow."

Orkin takes a pack of cigarettes out of his pants pocket, puts one of the cigarettes in his mouth, and lights it. He's playing it cagey now.

"As I understand about that body was lifted from the morgue wagon," he says, blowing out a mouthful of smoke, "according to the news stories them morgue guys that was there identified the other car that was involved was a Toyota Corolla. You remember it that way?"

"Yeah, that's what they said."

"Uh-huh. All right, now." Orkin has both elbows propped up on the table and he's squinting at the smoke rising from the tip of his cigarette. "Suppose I was to tell you a few days before Duane Vinton disappeared, he was observed driving a Toyota Corolla, and you understand nobody ever saw him driving a Toyota Corolla before. That ought to be worth something, wouldn't you say?"

"You've got more proof than just your say-so this is true?"

Orkin looks up, nods his head, a smug expression on his face. "So, like I said, information like that, wouldn't you say ought to be worth in the neighborhood of two Cs?" He thrusts a hand up in the air. "Wait! Before you answer that, let me add something to it. This talk we're having today could be just the first of many we maybe could have. Give me a little time, and we're doing business together, and maybe I can give you a line on where you can walk right in someplace and I wouldn't be surprised you find Vinton himself there, you understand?"

"In other words, you're saying you know where Vinton is, but before you finally tell me that, you want to squeeze me for all you can get, huh?"

"I didn't say that," Orkin says. "I wouldn't put it that way. We were talking about talks we're gonna have in the future. Right now, first, we got to settle up on this information I told you I could give you providing we get together on how much it's worth."

"All right, Benny, two Cs, and I think I'm getting robbed. But before you tell me, I want you to know I'm going to have to tell the cops—keeping you out of it."

Orkin nods. "I figured that already. I figured I can trust you to keep me out of it, I don't give a fuck you tell them."

"Let's hear it."

Orkin's sweating like a pig in August in Arkansas now as he says, "A couple of days before Vinton disappears, I'm leaving the spa after work one time and I'm walking out right behind Vinton and we're outside and he says, 'Come on, I'll give you a lift,' and we go over and he's got this Toyota Corolla parked there. Which is unusual and I remark on the car because I know he owns an MG and that's all I ever saw him driving before. And he says something about the Toyota belongs to a friend of his and he's only driving it for a couple of days."

Orkin pauses and lights another cigarette from the butt of the one he's been smoking. "So we get in the car, and before he drops me off, we stop at this gas station right around the corner from the spa on First Avenue and Vinton buys gas. Now, the thing is the guy that runs the gas station, he knows Vinton and he also remarks on the Toyota on account of he's used to seeing the MG and Vinton tells him the same thing about it's a friend's car and blah, blah. Vinton uses his credit card to pay for the gas, and that'd be another thing they'd have at the gas station. And also the guy that runs the gas station—his name's Hank Something. Vinton called him Hank. In addition to which, this Hank person is still at the gas station because I checked this morning to see he was, knowing I was going to be telling you all this later. Somebody can talk to him."

"And this happened exactly when?"

"Exactly one week ago day before yesterday." Orkin flicks the sweat out of his eyes. "What do you think, huh?"

"Okay, Benny. Here're the two C-bills. You better hope what you told me is worth them. And I don't want you pulling any sudden vanishing acts on me, either."

Orkin grabs the bills and stuffs them in his pants pocket. Then he lights another cigarette, letting the butt he's been holding drop into the plate of soupy gravy.

"Maybe you didn't hear me right on the phone," he says. "I ain't going nowhere. I wasn't handing you any snow job when I told you I was jammed—fucking—up. Two guys are out to get me, and they got enough clout to reach right into the police department and find out where I am if the cops know, you understand? I even quit my job at the place today."

"This have anything to do with what happened at the spa this morning?"

Orkin looks surprised. "You mean that guy that got drowned in the swimming pool? Oh, hell no, I don't know nothing about that. I swear on my mother's grave, Spanner."

"How about did Gregory Janish have anything to do with all this stuff with Jill Balfe and Duane Vinton?"

"Absolutely hell no!" Orkin says emphatically. "Janish and Vinton hated the other one's guts."

"All right, Benny, we'll leave it at that. When you have anything else to tell me, get in touch."

"Yeah," Orkin says eagerly. He reaches a hand toward the bottle of vodka on the table. "Hey, how about one for the road?"

"Ah, no, Benny. Another time maybe. But I did notice all those horse sheets on the bed. If you're not going anywhere, how come you're trying to handicap the horses?"

"Oh, sure, I'm playing the ponies. Gives me something to do while I'm holed up here. Ginger—my friend I told you about—she makes my bets for me around the corner at the OTB parlor."

Orkin moves to the door, does all the business of unshackling the police lock, then unlocks the door and opens it.

"Be seeing you," he says, his eyes casing the hallway in both directions before he slams the door again. Then there's the sound of him inside, locking up.

There's nobody in the elevator when it comes. Down in the lobby there's nobody behind the desk, either. The lobby's about the size of Benny Orkin's room and has about the same amount of charm. There's a girl standing at the entrance to the hotel. She's wearing a miniskirt that barely covers the curve of her buttocks, has boobs the size of tenpin bowling balls, and looks like she might be all of fifteen years old. She glances over and glances quickly away; she's already street-wise enough to suspect *vice cop* about any guy who fits the P.D. height and weight requirements.

It's almost dusk now outside. A hot, dry wind creates miniature whirlwinds among the debris littering the gutters alongside the curb. Looking west down 48th Street, you can see the fiery orange ball of sun setting behind the dark silhouette of the Palisades of New Jersey across the Hudson River.

Midway in the block is an outdoor phone booth.

On the inside of the glass door of the phone booth somebody's used a red crayon to scrawl a graffiti couplet:

N.Y.C. COPS
ARE TOPS

And then somebody else has used a black crayon to run a line through "TOPS" and has scrawled "FOPS."

The operator at the 16th Precinct puts the call through to Missing Persons and Hornstein answers, his words short and clipped, as if he's annoyed he has to answer the phone.

"This is J. T. Spanner again."

"Nothing new's come up since I talked to you, Spanner," he says curtly.

"Yeah, but I ran across some information I think you ought to know, sergeant."

"O-kay," he says resignedly. "What you got?"

"The source of this has to remain confidential. Agreed?"

"Agreed—depending upon if of course your source isn't criminally involved, but you know that."

"You remember the car that was used in the snatch of the body that might have been Jill Balfe's was identified as a Toyota Corolla?"

"I remember. And—?"

"From what I hear, Duane Vinton was seen driving a Toyota Corolla about two days before he disappeared."

Hornstein interrupts. "Vinton owned an MG. We checked that out."

"Which makes it even more interesting. From what I hear, Vinton told some people who saw him driving the Toyota that the Toyota was a friend's car. And from what I hear, you can possibly verify this with a witness and possibly even with some documentary evidence."

"Yeah, I'd sure like to know about that," Hornstein says slowly.

"All right, here it is: there's a filling station right around the corner on First Avenue from the health spa where Vinton worked. Late in the afternoon a week or so before the body was stolen from the morgue wagon, Vinton bought gas for the Toyota at that filling station. According to my information, the manager of the filling station, a man named Hank Somebody, knew Vinton and remarked on the fact that Vinton was driving a Toyota instead of the MG. Also, Vinton paid for the gas with a credit card. What do you think?"

"I'll have it all checked out," Hornstein says, a new crispness in his voice. "We'll see where it takes us."

"Yeah. That's sort of the way I felt, too. Oh, and there's one other thing. This afternoon I talked to those two Pan Am stewardesses who saw Jill Balfe at JFK that night. I showed them a copy of Duane Vinton's photograph, one of the ones that was recovered from Harry Flescher's office today and which Captain Tynan gave me. One of the stewardesses, Lillian Holm, thought she recognized Vinton as a man she'd seen at the airport night before last."

"With Jill Balfe?"

"No. But she says the man, if it was Vinton, was waiting for someone, possibly to come out of the U.S.-G. Airlines Building—"

Hornstein interrupts again: "But Jill Balfe never checked in at her office, remember—"

"The point is if the guy was Vinton and he was looking for Jill Balfe, he might not have known she wasn't in there, and he might have caught up with her later."

"Yeah, sure that's possible. It could have happened like that."

"Her identification was not positive, however."

"Still," Hornstein says. "Well, anything else?"

"No. That's all I have to report."

"Thanks, it could be a help, Spanner. I'll let you know what we uncover." He hangs up.

The next phone call is to the office. Ellie answers.

"What's doing, honey?"

"After that big flurry of activity this morning," Ellie says, "it's been quiet around here all afternoon. Lee's down at my place working on that typing you wanted done. Are you coming back in anymore today?"

"No, I don't expect to. Why don't you close up and go on home? I'll check with you or Lee in the morning."

"Okay, J. T. 'Bye."

Another dime, another phone call. This time there are nine rings at the other end of the line before Bobbie Gillian says, "Hello?"

"This is J. T. Spanner."

"Oh, hi! I thought maybe you'd forgotten me."

"Nope. How are you feeling now?"

"Uh, well, so-so." She pauses and then asks hesitantly, "Are you nearby, in the neighborhood? I thought, well, maybe you'd like a drink? I mean if you're not—if you don't have other plans."

"No, I'm free. Are you?"

"Yes, I am."

"I'll tell you what then: why don't I take you out to dinner instead?"

"All right," she says. "Yes, I'd like that."

"I'll pick you up about eight. Okay?"

"I'll be waiting. See you."

Thoughts often come unbidden to mind: Harry Flescher said last night, "I'd say one of those chicks—that Bobbie Gillian—goes for you, I could hear it in her voice. You could score with her, you know."

Horny thoughts.

. . . There are about 10,000 restaurants in Manhattan, 500 of them specializing in international foods. Italian restaurants lead the list, followed by French, Chinese, Spanish, Japanese, German, and Greek . . .

BOBBIE Gillian takes a sip of wine, smiles over the rim of the empty glass, and then sets the glass down on the table. "This is a nice place. Thank you for bringing me here, J. T."

She turns her head to glance around the restaurant, the main dining room of La Cocotte, on East 60th Street, opposite Bloomingdale's. It's a large, airy room which with its walls of glass windows and the profusion of plants and flowers that decorate the interior give it the appearance of an indoor garden.

When Bobbie turns her head to look around the room, other heads at the surrounding tables turn to look at her. She's worth a look. The burnished gold of her hair is set off nicely by her black chiffon evening dress. The dress is sleeveless and has a low-cut V-neck. She wears a gold necklace and gold earrings, two rings on the first and second fingers of her left hand, another ring on the first finger of her right hand—and how do women these days decide which fingers they're going to put rings on?

Turning back to the table, Bobbie says, "I like it here."

"I'm glad. There're just about two glasses of wine left in the bottle. Shall we finish it with our coffee?"

She nods and then says, "Yes, this is a nice place. I'd like to come here again."

"With all the dates I imagine you have, it was a challenge to choose a place where I hoped you hadn't been before and that you'd like."

She smiles and shakes her head. "I really don't run around *that* much, you know. Most people think stewardesses are out living it up every night of the week. I don't know where they get that idea."

"Sure you know where people get that idea. Because of your work. How many other single women in this town have an opportunity to meet as many men as you do?"

"Oh, yes," she says, nodding, "I have more opportunities, all right. But when you eliminate the unacceptables, it probably evens out to about the same number of dates any other single woman in New York City has."

"How do you decide who's unacceptable?"

"Are you asking me as an investigator working on a case—or what?" she asks, frowning.

"Or what. Right now I'm just a guy out on a date, like any other single guy in New York City."

"Okay, in that case I'll tell you that the unacceptables, which include *most* of the men you meet in this town, are one or another of the classic Four-Fs."

"Four-Fs? What're they?"

"Fags. Phonies. Fuck-ups. Phalluses. Phalluses—vulgarized—means they're just plain you-know-whats." She looks across the table, amused. "Am I shocking you, J. T.?"

"No. I just wonder if you aren't exaggerating a bit?"

"Well, if I am," she says, "so are practically all the single women in this town who've been around at all. To save themselves grief, they almost all use the Four-F classification when they meet and size up a man for the first time."

"So, how *do* you decide you'll go out with a guy? Me, for instance?"

She's smiling. "You said it right; *I* decide. Not the man. If a man comes on too strong when I meet him, I turn him off. If I decide I want to date him, I let him know it. Some men aren't secure enough to accept that. Obviously you were—you are, because that's the way it happened with us."

She pauses for a moment and then says, "And of course there's the matter of what you'd call—vibes, I guess. Oh, hey, that reminds me: what's your sign?"

"My sign of what?"

"You know, your zodiac sign."

"Oh, that. I was born January seventeenth. Capricorn, would that be right?"

"Capricorn, yes." She nods. "That figures. 'Steady, determined, loyal, an achiever.' Capricorn; that's why we're compatible. Capricorn and Libra go well together. They fit each other. I'm a Libra."

"Come on, how do you know all that stuff? Is that all true or are you making it up?"

"Some of it's true." She laughs. "The rest of it I made up."

"You must have made up the part about Capricorn and Libra going well together. Because I remember a case once—a guy named Herman Krause. A mass murderer. Killed a dozen women. Their bodies were found with valentines on their breasts and Krause had killed them with a bow and arrow, the arrows shot through the valentines into the bodies. Turned out all the victims were Libras. They called it 'The Libra Murders.' After they arrested Krause, they checked his birthdate and discovered he was a Capricorn. Quite a famous case."

Her eyes are very wide. "Is that true or did you make it up?"

"Some of it's true. There was a murderer I remember named Herman Krause. He killed some guy. I made up the rest of it."

She shakes her head. "Oh *you!* You're putting me on. If I'm ever going to get to know you, I have to find out what's important to you."

"You really want to know? Okay, it's important to me to try to find your missing roommate—that's what I'm getting paid for. And that body on the bridge, it bugs me. Who she was, who killed her, and why."

"Do you think it was Jill's body?"

"I don't know. It doesn't matter. I mean, even if it turns out Jill Balfe is alive and well, I'd still want to know about the body. Things like that, I consider to be my business, too, whether I get paid for it or not. Do you understand what I mean?"

"I'm not sure," she says slowly.

"All right, look at it this way: most days it's enough for me to get from here, this moment, to there, the future—whatever it is—with a minimum of flak, with enough money to live reasonably decently, with small pleasures along the way. Once in a while, there's the bonus of a case solved. Most of them aren't all that earth-shattering, but satisfying just the same. Now there's this thing about the body on the bridge. An unidentifiable corpse, tortured and mutilated. The sheer—enigma—of the incident. Yes, I want the answers. That's why I do what I do. It's not all just the money."

"You like what you do, then, huh?" she asks.

"Yeah, most of the time. It's—well, did you ever play poker? Stud poker? Do you know how it's played?"

"I know how it's played, yes." Bobbie nods.

"You see, a good satisfying case is like when you're playing, in a really high-stakes stud game, five-card or seven-card. Most of the cards you're playing against show on the board, but some of the cards are hidden, face-down. So, part of the time you're trying to evaluate every card you can see—even if the card eventually turns out to have no importance. The rest of the time, you're playing blindly against the cards you can't see. Sometimes there's bluffing, there's desperation, there's true strength behind those hidden cards. You're trying to figure it all out in your head, playing hunches, instinct, hoping for some luck. You win a few, you lose a few, and you know that that's the way it is."

"I think I understand," she says. "You talked about your future—well, I can tell your fortune. Don't laugh. Hold out your palm."

She bends her head, her finger tracing lightly over the lines and creases imprinted there. "H'mm," she whispers, "you have a long life-line, that's good. Let's see, yes, there are the two broken lines; your divorces. Yes, you're going to have a long, happy life."

Her finger remains, the tip of the nail of her index finger lightly tickling the palm as she looks up. "Would you like to come back to the apartment for a nightcap?"

"If I understand your explanation of the way things are in the world nowadays, I guess that's my cue to answer: I thought you'd never ask. The answer is yes."

She laughs.

**ALL
VISITORS
MUST
BE
ANNOUNCED**

———*Sign inside entrance at 600 East 38th Street*

THE luminous dial on the Sheffield boudoir clock on the small table next to the head of the bed shows the time to be a few seconds after 12:15 A.M. Bobbie Gillian has left the door slightly ajar, and soft light from the living room spills like a phosphorous wave across the bedroom carpeting. There's a whisper of music distantly from the living-room stereo, and the bedroom is awash in the cool, refreshing flow from the air conditioner and the scent of her Au Courant perfume.

She comes into the room. For a moment, walking toward the bed from the doorway, she's backlighted by the illumination from the living room, the shapely curves of her body outlined through the lacy peach-colored negligee.

"You're beautiful, Bobbie."

She smiles as she stands by the bed and lets her negligee fall to her feet. The soft light reflects the sheen of her smooth, faintly pink skin and, there and there, the burnished blonde hair.

There's a teasing look on her face but her eyes are serious as she slides onto the silk bedsheets, braced on her knees. Her face is close, above. Her kisses are playful, creating little tingling sensations where they touch and arouse nerve endings. Soon the kisses are probing, and there's a stillness in the room. Staring down wide-eyed, she lowers herself slowly. There's a feel of moist, tender flesh against flesh, the folds of those lips parting, encircling and, after a time, there's a flutter, a quiver, they open and inside is velvety wetness, time is suspended . . .

After a long, drifting while, Bobbie eases herself off onto the bed, squirms near, and cuddles close.

"J. T.?"

"Mm?"

"I feel good."

"I'm glad. I do, too."

She's quiet for a moment. Then she says, "Ask you something?"

"Mm?"

"What don't you like about—you know, being married?"

"Hell, I like it. The fact that I've tried it twice so far ought to prove that."

"No. Seriously, J. T."

"Seriously? Mm. Well, maybe it's because you can only be married to one person at a time, and that sort of limits the search."

"The search for what?"

"The search for what everybody wants."

"What's that?"

"Why, the perfect fuck, of course."

She laughs. "You're terrible. Come on now, be serious. Are you still friendly with your two ex-wives? How do you feel about them?"

"Bobbie, this may come as a surprise to you but they both work for me. How do I feel about them? They're both very special people to me. What the hell, they both still have the same qualities that attracted me to them in the beginning. I don't personally believe that old saying that friendship—or love—should end with marriage, or divorce. In my life, at least, there just haven't been that many special people."

"I think I like that," she says. She snuggles up and is soon asleep.

The apartment is silent, the soothing cool flow from the air conditioner drifts across the bed, the room is dark; sleep is only the blink of an eye away—and then, almost imperceptibly at first and soon more disturbingly, some kind of light from somewhere outside the window plays across the bedroom ceiling. The light doesn't go away.

The carpet is soft and yielding under bare feet. Bobbie doesn't stir on the bed.

At the window the view, looking down, is of an alleyway in back of the apartment building. The light reflected on the bedroom ceiling comes from an open doorway at ground level. A car is parked in the alley, backed up to within a yard or so from the lighted doorway. Two men are carrying the limp body of a girl toward the car. One of the men is unmistakably Gregory Janish.

There's no time to dress except for pants, double-checking to make sure the .357 Magnum is securely in the holster clipped to the belt. Bobbie is still sleeping peacefully.

Outside her apartment door, there's a fire-exit door at the rear of the hallway.

The concrete stairs end four flights down at a door which opens out into the back alley.

The car is still there in the alley. It's a four-year-old dusty brown Plymouth Gold Duster with New Jersey license plates 59899724.

The girl's body is lying in the alley near the rear of the car. The car's trunk lid is up. There's no sign of Gregory Janish. The other guy who was helping carry the girl's body a few minutes earlier is trying to drag the body toward the trunk of the car, clutching the body by the armpits. He looks up startled when he sees and hears the fire-exit door open. He lets the body fall and turns and runs toward the front of the car. He scrambles into the front seat, guns the motor and, with the trunk lid still up, the Plymouth roars down the alley with a scream of tires and disappears.

Light from the fire-exit door falls across the body of the girl. She's about 5'7" and scrawny thin. Her age is maybe eighteen, nineteen, and she has streaked blonde hair that needs washing and coloring. She's wearing a blouse, a skirt, and sandals. She has no detectable heartbeat or pulse, her skin is a sickly white, and the whole body is rigid from what is called cadaveric spasm which frequently occurs at the moment of death and is similar to but precedes rigor mortis. Her eyes are closed. Under the lids, the pupils of her eyes have contracted to pinpoints. There are fresh needle tracks on the underside of her left arm; older, fainter scars in the same area of her right arm.

It's silent in the alleyway and almost all the windows in the rear of the apartment building are dark except for a couple of windows on the higher floors. The patch of sky visible above the top of the apartment building is black and starless. Dank smog floats in the hot night air.

A few paces up the alley, there's light showing around the frame of the not-quite-closed rear door to The Good Health Spa.

The door is heavy metal. Up close, there's not enough space between the door and the frame to see inside. The door pulls open soundlessly. There's only a single light on in the interior of the spa and it's at the near end of the pool just inside the door. The light shines down on the concrete edge of the pool and out over the water for a distance of three or four feet.

There are a couple of small bundles, six or seven inches square and wrapped in what look like waterproof casings, stacked on the concrete edge of the pool. Next to them is a wadded-up towel. Beyond the circle of light the whole place is in shadows and eerily hushed.

Suddenly there's a loud splash, and a figure surfaces in the water and hooks an arm up over the concrete edge of the pool. It's Gregory Janish. Water cascades from his dripping hair, and he's wearing diving goggles.

"Just hold it right there, Janish."

Janish's head snaps up and he looks stunned as his eyes focus on the Magnum aimed straight at his chest. His right hand lifts slowly and shoves the goggles up on top of his head.

"What the hell—?" he says. "How'd you get in here?"

"You forgot and left the door open. But let's talk about something else. Like a dead girl lying out in the alley. O.D.'d, I'd say, and about what's in those packages there by the pool. Heroin, I'd say—just like what must have been the massive fix in her body."

"What the hell you talking about?" There's fear on his face but he's going to try to bluff it out. "What dead girl in the alley? What heroin? Those?" He points to the stacked bundles on the concrete. "I never saw those packages before. You plant them there? You trying to frame me?"

"Save it for the cops, Janish."

"You're not a cop?" he asks. He's confused. "What—who—?"

"A private investigator."

"So it's your word against mine."

"Yeah, I guess so, Janish. The thing is maybe I should just kill you right now. Like you killed Harry Flescher last night. I talked to Flescher a while before he was killed. He knew you were up to something. He was right about you."

"You're not going to kill anybody," Janish says. "And nobody's pinning any raps on me for anything. Look, can I for Christ's sake get out of the pool before my balls get waterlogged?"

"Come on, slow and easy."

He pulls himself up to the deck of the pool, lifts his goggles off, and shakes his head, spraying water from side to side, his eyes blinking. He's wearing purple swim trunks. He makes a motion toward the wadded-up towel lying at his feet. "Okay if I dry my face?"

"Go ahead."

He reaches down and picks up the towel. A bright orange flash explodes through the cloth as he fires the revolver hidden inside the towel. The blast of the gunshot reverberates around the interior of the spa as if it were an echo chamber. The bullet thuds into the frame of the rear door.

There's a look of panicked amazement on Janish's face in the split-second before the .357 slug from the Magnum smashes into the bridge of his nose, blowing away the top half of his face and skull, and scattering bits of cartilage, bone fragments, bloody mucus and tissue across the concrete pool deck and out over the surface of the water. Janish falls hard, sprawled on his back, what's left of his head twisted to one side. He was probably dead before he hit the concrete.

The nearest phone is on the desk in the glass-enclosed office across from where Janish is lying.

Dial 911.

"Police operator."

"I want to report a fatal shooting at Number Six Hundred East Thirty-Eighth Street in a place called The Good Health Spa."

"Six-zero-zero East Three-eighth Street, The Good Health Spa. Who—?"

"My name is J. T. Spanner. I'm a private investigator. I fired the fatal shot in self-defense. There's also a dead female subject in the alley behind Number Six Hundred East Thirty-eighth Street. She died, I think, from an overdose of drugs. Tell your cars to come to the back alley at this address. I'll be waiting there."

"You stay there," the police operator says in a clipped voice and hangs up.

Two cigarettes later, three squad cars and an unmarked dark blue Ford Fairlane turn into the alley and roll to a stop a few feet from the dead girl. The cars have come with sirens off but with red flasher lights on the car roofs rotating, splattering color, garish as crimson paint, up and down the alley and across the body.

Six uniformed patrolmen are the first ones out of the cars, hands on their revolvers. They wait at a distance until the two plainclothesmen emerge from the unmarked car. The plainclothesmen cross in front of the headlights from the cars. They're the cops from 16th Homicide—the black one, Sergeant Royston, and his partner, Sergeant Haas. Haas stops to look at the dead girl. Royston strolls over.

"Uh-huh, Mr. Spanner," he says. He nods his head. "You're certainly dressed appropriately for the weather."

"I was visiting a friend upstairs in the building when all this started—if you want to hear about it."

"We'll get to that. I was just making a small pleasantry."

"It's too hot tonight, sergeant, too late, and one dead body too many for me to appreciate small pleasantries."

"Sure, I can understand how you feel." He looks around at the girl's body, looks back again, and says, "Speaking of dead bodies, I understand there's another one somewhere around here."

"Inside. I'll show you."

"Uh, there's just one thing first, Mr. Spanner. That gun in your holster, mind giving it to me?"

Royston takes the Magnum by the barrel and sticks it in his waistband under his jacket. He beckons to a couple of the patrolmen and they follow along behind into the spa.

Inside the door, the sergeant goes ahead to the edge of the pool and leans down on one knee beside Gregory Janish's body. The two uniformed cops stand watchfully until

Royston comes back over. He takes a notebook and ballpoint pen out of his coat pocket.

"Before we talk," he says, "you know I have to recite you the Miranda ruling: you have a right to a lawyer before you make any statement. If you don't have a lawyer, we'll provide you with one. And understand that I'm warning you now that anything you tell me can also be used against you in court."

"I understand. I'm offering my statement voluntarily."

Royston looks over at the body. "The victim was—?"

"Gregory Janish. He managed this place."

Royston, writing in the notebook, nods. He says, "Go ahead."

"I was upstairs, visiting in a friend's apartment. One of the windows there looks out on the alley. There was a light coming from the alley. I went to the window to investigate the source of the light. The light was coming from the open rear door to this spa. I could see a car parked in the alley and two men. The men were carrying the body of a girl from the direction of the door of the spa in the direction of the car. I recognized Gregory Janish as one of the men from having seen him yesterday when you and Sergeant Haas brought me here. I did not recognize the other man. I put on my pants and came down to investigate. When I—"

"Hold it!" Royston says, frowning. "This friend of yours upstairs observed everything in the alley that you did?"

"No. She was asleep."

"I see." He sighs softly. "Go on."

"When I got downstairs, Janish had disappeared. The other man was trying to drag the body to the car. The lid to the trunk of the car was raised. The man appeared to see and hear me as soon as I stepped into the alley. He left the body, ran for the car, and escaped."

"Did you get a look at this man?"

"Fleetingly. He was slightly more than medium height,

I'd say, not too heavy, and my impression was that he was a younger man."

"And the car?" There's a faint note of bored disbelief in Royston's voice now. "I don't suppose you had a chance to get a description of it, either, huh?"

"Yeah, as a matter of fact, I did. The car was a four-year-old dusty brown Plymouth Gold Duster."

Royston glances up from this notebook with a look of mild surprise on his face.

"Another thing you might want to note, sergeant. The car had New Jersey plates, and the license number was NJP 319."

The sergeant shakes his head; he wasn't expecting that information. "You mind giving me those numbers again, Mr. Spanner?" he asks. He's paying closer attention to the answers now.

"New Jersey NJP 319."

"Please continue."

"I took a close look at the girl's body. It was my opinion, from the rigid condition of the body, the contraction of the eyeball pupils, the needle tracks on her arms, that she'd died from an overdose of drugs."

"You're quite sure she was dead at that time?"

"Positive."

"All right. And so then what happened?"

"I glanced around the alley. I noticed that that door there, at the back of the spa, wasn't completely closed. I came over to the door and looked inside. I couldn't see anything. The light that's on now was on then. I opened the door and came inside. There was nobody here that I could see. Those packages over by the edge of the pool were right where they are now. The towel there by the body was at that time lying next to the packages, wadded up. I stood looking around the place for maybe two, three, seconds, and then there was a splashing sound in the pool and Gregory Janish surfaced in the water. He was wearing those diving goggles there. I pulled my gun and aimed it at him. He appeared stunned at seeing me. I told him about the body in the alley, I accused him of dealing in drugs, which I think is in those packages, and I accused him of killing Harry Flescher here yesterday morning."

Sergeant Royston raises a hand. "And what did he say in answer to those accusations?"

"He denied them, of course. He was already plotting his legal defense. He claimed he'd never seen those packages before and that I'd planted them here."

"You didn't touch them, did you?"

"Nothing's been touched, sergeant."

"All right. So what happened next?"

"He—Janish—asked me if he could get out of the pool. I said he could. He climbed out. Then he asked me if he could use his towel to dry off. I said he could. He picked up the towel. He fired a shot through the towel, from a gun hidden under the towel. The shot missed me. I think you'll find the bullet embedded in the door frame back there. I then shot him. I didn't miss. I then called the police."

"Janish still have his gun in his hand when you shot him?"

"That's right."

"And how many shots did you fire?"

"One."

"Do you have anything else to add?"

"No."

"Then I have just one more question," Royston says. "This friend of yours that you were visiting upstairs, I'm going to need the name and apartment number."

"Her name's Barbara Gillian and it's Apartment 4J."

"You understand we're going to have to talk to her."

"Yeah."

Sergeant Royston closes his notebook and rubs his jaw. "You know you're going to have to stick around for a while."

"I know."

He nods. "Captain Tynan'll want to be in on this one. I'm going to try to contact him."

"Sure. You don't mind if I wait outside in the alley, do you? I've had it with this place."

"I don't mind. You want a cigarette?"

"Thanks. I have some."

Outside now, the alley's jammed with squad cars and cops who have responded to the dispatcher's call. Sergeant Royston goes over to his car and gets on the radio. Nobody's said anything about anybody being in police custody, but the two uniformed patrolmen who were in the spa now stand guard a couple of feet away. There are lights on in windows all over the apartment building, and you can see people leaning out of most of the lighted windows, looking down at the scene in the alley. The body of the dead girl is still lying where it was, awaiting the arrival of the M.E.

The squawk from a dozen police radios creates a babel of sound in the canyonlike confines of the alleyway:

"Signal ten-thirteen, Twenty-nine West—"

"Unit Eleven calling Central—"

"Assist patrolman. Repeat signal thirteen—"

"—prowler at—"

"Twenty-five to Central—"

"—what units responding? K."

"Ten-four—"

"Ten-one to Fifteen Edward. Respond."

"—Park Avenue, gunshots—"

"—Was that a signal thirteen?"

"—suspected perpetrator on roof—"

"—responding. K."

"Signal thirteen. Armed man at —"

"K."

"—Ten-four."

"—Ten-five that transmission—"

"Ten-thirteen! Cop shot! Ten-thirteen!"

"—send emergency equipment!"
"—Ten-thirteen! Cop shot! Cop—"
"Six-zero Baker to Central. K."
"—shot!"
"This is a Ten-thirteen."
"—Central—"
"—signal—"
"—unit—"
"K."
"—respond—"
"Central? Are you receiving—?"

Following is the transcription of a tape-recorded statement taken this date from Private Investigator J. T. Spanner at the 16th Precinct, New York, N. Y.
Present: Captain John Tynan
Homicide Division . . .

—*16th Precinct typed transcript*

OUTSIDE the window of the interrogation room, the sky to the east is a predawn pale gray. The three streetlights in view along the block in front of the 16th Precinct are still burning. Inside the room, under the light from the ceiling globe, tattered cobwebs of cigarette and cigar smoke spin in the air.

John Tynan is sitting tilted back in a wooden armchair, his feet braced against the windowsill. He's in his shirt-sleeves, his tie is pulled loose, he needs a shave, and his eyes are red-rimmed. Sergeant Royston is sitting on the edge of a table in the center of the room, Sergeant Haas is leaning against a far wall, both looking equally exhausted, and Inspector Max Kauffman is pacing up and down the room. He's only arrived in the past half-hour, and he's freshly shaved and looks rested. All four of the men are reading copies of the typed transcript. Once in a while one or another of the men glances over, then resumes reading.

In the past hours, the police have tracked down the owner of the Plymouth Gold Duster with New Jersey license plates NJP 319. He's a twenty-four-year-old known drug addict and unemployed sheet-metal worker named Peter Stargen who lives in Perth Amboy, New Jersey. He's been taken into custody by police. Stargen has identified the dead girl in the alley as a Janet Shimkin, nineteen years old, who is also a known addict and unemployed. Stargen has told police that he and Janet Shimkin lived together in Perth Amboy. Stargen has also confessed that the girl received her fatal fix of heroin from Gregory Janish in The Good Health Spa. In addition, Stargen has testified that Janish has been supplying him and the girl with drugs for a period of two years. From statements made by Stargen, police believe they can tie Stargen and the girl to a series of armed robberies committed in New Jersey over the past couple of years.

Meanwhile in the past hours, police have recovered a cache of heroin from the spa. The heroin, wrapped in waterproof casing, was hidden in the side of the spa swimming pool, below the waterline, in a hollowed-out space which Janish apparently usually kept covered by a removable tile except when he was taking the drugs out or returning them to the hiding place.

Inspector Max Kauffman finally stops pacing and tosses the copy of the transcript he's been reading onto the table. "All right, Spanner," he says. "Your signed statement seems to hold up. A couple of points here and there I'm not completely satisfied with, but—" He glances around the room. "Anybody have any questions?"

Captain Tynan, Sergeant Royston, and Sergeant Haas all shake their heads.

"Does that mean I'm free to go, inspector?"

"Not yet, Spanner," the inspector says. "I want to talk to you in my office. I want you there, too, captain."

Tynan nods.

"Royston, you and Haas are dismissed," Max Kauffman says and strides from the room. Royston and Haas leave, too, and Tynan stands, rubbing his back.

"Okay, Spanner," he says then, "let's go."

Outside the interrogation room, in the area of the booking desk, there's a row of benches. Bobbie Gillian is sitting on one of the benches. Her slacks and blouse look as if they were pulled on hastily. There are dark smudges of fatigue under her eyes, and she looks forlorn. She jumps up and hurries over, an expression of anxiousness on her face.

"Are you all right, J. T.?"

"I'm okay, honey. I'm sorry they had to bring you in to make a statement. I thought you'd have gone on back home by now."

She shakes her head. "I was waiting for you. I wanted to make sure they were going to release you. Can you take me home now?"

"No. I'm going to be here a little while longer yet. Why don't you go on home and get some rest? I'll call you later."

She backs away and sits down on the bench again. "No, I'm going to wait for you," she says firmly.

"Okay. I should be down soon."

Tynan has been waiting a couple of paces away. Now he turns to walk on down the hall.

"She seems like a nice girl," he says.

"Yeah."

Tynan doesn't say anything else on the ride in the elevator to the third floor.

The inspector's office is in a corner of the station house. There's nobody on duty at the desk outside the office. The door is closed. Tynan raps and opens the door.

Max Kauffman is sitting at his desk. The office has paneled oak walls and exposed oak beams running across the ceiling, the wood gleaming richly brown in soft, indirect lighting that comes from fixtures recessed in the ceiling and the tops of the windows. Thick pile carpeting, a deep gold color, covers the floor from wall to wall, and matching gold drapes are pulled across the windows. A collection of abstract oil paintings hangs on the walls and pieces of sculpture stand on low pedestal tables illuminated by soft light. There's a stone fireplace in one wall, an air conditioner in another. The inspector sits behind a massive mahogany desk in a swivel armchair covered in leather. The desk is so shiny the lights reflect in its surface. There are other leather-covered armchairs arranged in front of the desk. At the opposite end of the room is a long leather-covered sofa and several more chairs set around a mahogany coffee table. On the coffee table is a crystal vase filled with chrysanthemums. The room is cool and smells of rich leather and oil polish.

"Sit down, sit down," Max Kauffman says, gesturing toward the chairs in front of his desk. He lights a cigar. Tynan takes out a package of cigarettes and then puts them back in his pocket without lighting up.

The inspector swings around in his chair. "Tell me something, Spanner. Did you really have to shoot the sonofabitch through the head, blow him away? I happen to know you're a crack shot."

"Look, inspector, he was holding a gun on me. He'd already taken one shot at me—"

"Yeah, yeah, yeah. It's messy, though."

"I can't help that, inspector. Everything happened the way I told you it happened. For Christ's sake, you've even got that junkie witness, Stargen, to verify ninety-nine percent of what I've told you."

"All that aside," Max Kauffman says, "the whole thing's still going to look fishy to the D.A. Just consider the way he's going to review the facts. That character—Flescher—is found floating in the pool of the health spa. We're investigating what happened. The manager of the spa—Janish—is certainly a possible suspect if there was a murder. We find out you and Flescher have been together. Flescher's dead, so all we have to go on is your side of that encounter. Then you shoot Janish. You say it was in self-defense. Janish is dead, so all we have to go on is your side of what happened. The point is: you show up looking for a girl who disappeared a couple of days ago, and right away a couple of people die. It's going to bug the D.A. It's messy."

"It might not seem so messy if we put the whole thing into perspective, you know."

"Meaning what?"

"Meaning Janish would still be alive today and peddling drugs, and Flescher would also still be alive, if two people—Jill Balfe and Duane Vinton, who had had some connection with the spa—hadn't disappeared."

Max Kauffman takes a puff on his cigar, frowning. "You're theorizing then that their disappearance is somehow connected to what Janish was doing, the drug stuff?"

"No, actually, I'm not. There's still no evidence of that. Although it's possible. What I am saying is that if Flescher hadn't been hired to find one of those missing persons and me the other, none of us—Flescher, Janish, or me—would have known the other existed."

Captain Tynan, who hasn't spoken up to this point, now says, "All right, Spanner, let's talk about those two missing persons for a minute. Suppose you try to hypothesize a connection between their disappearance and Janish, to see where that gets us."

"Since I've never tried to do that, I'd rather repeat something I told you once before. Harry Flescher *was* convinced there was a connection. Remember? He said he suspected there was something going on at the spa and that Jill Balfe and Duane Vinton were either involved in it or found out about it, and because of that were missing or dead. And don't forget: at the time Flescher had those suspicions, he didn't know about Janish's drug trafficking, as we do now."

"All right, then," Max Kauffman says irritably, "where's the proof of any of this?"

"I'm sorry, inspector. I'm not making my point clear—"

"Then, for Christ's sakes, make it clear."

"The point is that maybe their disappearance had nothing to do with Janish's drug business. But because they disappeared, and had a connection with the spa, it focused attention on the spa. That led Flescher to his theory, and he plunged headlong into an investigation of Janish and the spa. Just doing that alone would have been enough to get him killed since Janish *was* a drug dealer and had to protect his activities. The same thing applies to why he tried to kill me."

"Uh-huh," Tynan says slowly. "What you're saying is that all the time there could have been two separate cases going on here: one, the disappearances; and the other, Janish's drug dealing. The disappearances just coincidentally led to Janish's activities. That it?"

"Yeah, I'm saying it's a possibility. Although, of course, there's also a possibility there's a connection between the two."

"All right, then," Max Kauffman says, "for the moment, let's consider them as separate cases, and let's assume that the Janish case is now closed. Where does that leave us with the two disappearances?"

"Precisely where we started," Tynan says dryly. "Isn't that what you'd say, Spanner?"

"Maybe not precisely, captain. You both know, don't you, that I informed Sergeant Hornstein that I'd uncovered some possible evidence that Duane Vinton may have been at the airport the night Jill Balfe disappeared. And that I also told Hornstein that Vinton had been observed driving a Toyota before the time that the body was found and stolen—by two individuals in a Toyota?"

Tynan nods. "Sergeant Hornstein reported that information to me last evening, and I advised the inspector. The department's going to check it out. There's only one thing that bothers us, Spanner."

"Yeah?"

"We know you say one of those Pan Am stewardesses told you she thinks she saw Vinton at the airport, and we'll talk to her but"—Tynan leans forward—"we're curious about your source for the other piece of information."

"As I told Sergeant Hornstein, the source is confidential."

"You aren't going to make us lean on you, are you?" Inspector Kauffman asks in a flat voice.

"I have no evidence that my source is criminally involved. And I'm certainly not withholding evidence from you."

The inspector smiles tightly. "You could be flirting with possible obstruction of justice."

"Nope, I don't think so. Of course, if we're going to have a big legal hassle over the issue, I'll have to let my lawyer do the talking for me."

Max Kauffman's face flushes a dark red. For a moment, he appears ready to blow his top. Then he takes a puff on his cigar and says in a deadly quiet voice, "All right, Spanner. We'll let the issue ride for now. But God help you if it turns out you've played fast and loose with us. I warned you before: don't try to play cop on your own."

"The way I see it, I'm only trying to serve the best interests of my client. As a licensed investigator, I believe I'm operating within my rights—unless they've changed the laws since the last time I heard."

Max Kauffman shrugs. "Uh-huh. Well, the D.A. may see it differently. And so may you when you get into the coroner's inquest, or maybe even get called before a grand jury."

"If and when that happens, I imagine my lawyer would advise me to plead privilege."

The inspector waves a hand in the air. "All right, Spanner, you've always had to be so fucking hard-nosed, go on, get out of here. For now. We'll notify you when ballistics releases your gun."

Captain Tynan gives a brief nod of his head. He stays behind in Max Kauffman's office.

The third-floor corridor is filled with police officers now since it's change-of-shift time in the precinct. When the elevator comes, Sergeant Murray Hornstein gets off.

"Spanner," he says, and looks surprised.

"Yeah. Hello, sergeant."

"I just finished reading the report of that ruckus you were in last night," Hornstein says. "There was a note for me to see the inspector first thing I got in. You been with him. Am I right?"

"Uh-huh."

"You okay?" Hornstein's face is sympathetic.

"I guess."

Hornstein scratches his ear. "That business last night—does it affect the Jill Balfe case any?"

"Damned if I know, sergeant. I don't think so, though. The inspector and the captain may have other opinions."

"Listen," Hornstein says, "I appreciate the information you gave me yesterday. We're going to get cracking on it—you know what I mean?"

"Good. Uh-huh."

"Another thing," Hornstein says, "I still don't have a report from the morgue yet on that body they found in the Queens sewer. Soon as I do, I'll let you know."

"Thanks, sergeant."

"Take it easy," he says and goes on toward Max Kauffman's office.

Down on the first floor of the station house, Bobbie Gilian is still sitting on one of the benches near the booking desk.

She looks worn out but she manages a smile as she stands. "Can we go home now, J. T.?"

"Yeah, come on, baby."

There's a haze across the sky this morning. During the night, sanitation trucks have washed down the streets and the pavement outside the station house is still wet. A

"Captain Hook"—the epithet Manhattan motorists have given to police tow trucks which cruise the city and haul away illegally parked cars on the streets—is pulling out from the curb in front of the precinct building. There are no taxicabs in sight.

Bobbie slips off one of her sandals and rubs the bottom of her foot. "The police know you had to do what you did last night—don't they, J. T.?" she asks. "They aren't going to make trouble for you, are they?"

"I don't know, honey. I think it's going to be all right, though."

Bobbie looks up. "You're coming home with me, aren't you? You need to rest. You look so tired."

"I *am* tired. But I can't take time out right now. I'm going to drop you off. Then I'm going home and change clothes. I've got some business to attend to. How about I call you later?"

"I haven't had a chance to tell you," she says. "I have a flight out to Chicago tonight. I'll be there overnight and come back in the morning. Can you call me tomorrow or I'll call you, and maybe we can get together tomorrow night?"

"Okay, fine."

An empty taxicab finally appears up the street. As it angles over to stop, Bobbie says, "J. T.?"

"Huh?"

"You—you don't think Jill was mixed up with any of that drug stuff at the spa, do you?"

"That's the business I've got to attend to. There's a guy I want to get some answers from."

> REPORT 2nd DEATH
> AT EAST SIDE HEALTH SPA
> Police are investigating the death of the manager of an East Side health spa who was shot and killed by a local private investigator early today, the second death to occur in the spa within the past 24 hours. The victim was Gregory Stefan Janish . . .
>
> ——*Late City Edition, the* New York Post

GINGER Higget is 5′6″ or 5′7″ in her bare feet, and has frizzy blonde hair. Her face, overlaid by a fast-hardening veneer of dissipation and bad cosmetics, probably won't look much different twenty years from now when she's in her fifties. She's still got a good body, though, and from the way she moves, jiggling tits and ass, you know she knows it. She's wearing bright orange hip-huggers and a sleeveless blue cotton blouse.

Earlier, there's been a whole *megillah* of:
pounding on the hotel door
and: "Who's there?"
and: "I'm J. T. Spanner. I want to talk to Benny."
and: hurried whispering at a distance inside the room
and: the rattle and clanking of the door being unlocked

Now, while she's relocking the door, she motions to the chairs at the table in the middle of the room and says, "Why don't you sit down? Benny'll be right out."

Almost as if it's on cue, there's the sound of a toilet flushing in the bathroom, and Benny Orkin opens the door and comes into the room. He's still wearing the same gray twill slacks he had on yesterday and is in his undershirt and socks. He has a .45 automatic stuck in the back of the waistband of his slacks.

"Didn't I hear something about you on the radio this morning?" he asks. "Something about a shooting or something?"

"I want to talk to you, Benny. Alone."

"You got it, man." He thrusts a hand into his pants pocket, pulls out some bills and hands them to Ginger Higget. "Here, sweetie, go play some horses for me. A six-four-three triple in the ninth at Belmont."

She takes the money, mumbles some unintelligible words, wiggles her feet into a pair of frayed huaraches and, after Benny unlocks the door, goes out. He locks up again and turns.

"You ever see anything like that ass, hers?" he says proudly. "And the head she gives, I wouldn't bullshit you—she could suck water out of a rock."

"Yeah, well, that's interesting all right, Benny. Listen, sit down, will you? You and I have got some serious talking to do."

He pulls the other chair out from the table and sits. "You got trouble with the cops, huh, over killing Janish?"

"We both got trouble, Benny. Me. And you, if you don't give me some straight answers."

Orkin's starting to sweat, but he says indignantly, "What you mean—straight answers is what I been giving you."

"Not about Janish, you haven't. You had to know he was dealing drugs."

He shrugs. "So, who's denying it? I knew, yeah. He tried to play it close to his vest but I caught wise, you understand? I don't think he ever suspected I knew, though. So I knew, so what? It had nothing to do with me. I might do a little of this, a little of that, you understand, but I wouldn't personally buy, sell, or use none of that drug shit. Look, you know my whole rap sheet for—what, fifteen years now—there's nothing on there about no narcotics. What Janish did—'' He shrugs.

"Let's get back to what I'm really interested in, Benny, and that's the disappearance of Jill Balfe and/or Duane Vinton—now, are you going to sit there and try to tell me that whatever happened to them had nothing to do with Janish and his dope peddling?"

"That's what I'm telling you," he says, nodding his head.

"That's not the way I see it, Benny. Let me spell it out for you the way I see it: Janish was dealing drugs; that we know. What's a good way to get drugs? Smuggle them into the country, right? For that, you need somebody who's in and out of the country a lot, right? An airline stewardess, maybe, right? And how do you get an airline stewardess— like Jill Balfe, maybe—to do that kind of work for you? You use a stud like Duane Vinton, right? It all ties together, Benny, you understand?"

"I can see how you might put it together that way," Orkin says slowly, "but it'd sure be a hard way to do it, considering the fact that the kind of operation Janish was running was strictly small potatoes. He wasn't pushing that much, and he was a pusher, not a supplier. For what he needed, all he'd have to do is take a walk to any one of a hundred spots in town and make a wholesale buy. That'd be an awful lot of trouble to go to, I mean, smuggling it in from across the ocean—"

"I still think—"

Orkin shakes his head violently, highly agitated. "No! No! No! You're way off base, man, what you think."

"How can you be so positive unless you know what did happen to Vinton and Jill Balfe?"

"You're crowding me now, man," Benny says, and adds plaintively, "We never did business this way before—"

"Knock off the crap, Benny. This isn't like before. The cops are crowding *me*. I've got to know for a fact that the disappearances of Jill Balfe and Duane Vinton weren't somehow tied to Janish and the drugs, with maybe you in there somewhere, too."

Orkin starts to say something, hesitates, and licks his lips as he says, "When the cops had you in there asking you how come you shot Janish and all, did you mention any of this—what you think—to them?"

"No. Not yet. I don't tell them everything I think, they don't tell me everything they think. But I imagine the same thoughts have crossed their minds—they're not stupid. Where I got my neck stuck out is I'm protecting you—"

"Look! Look! Look!" Orkin says. "We talking about where are the broad and Vinton, and we're talking about Janish and drugs. So, for a fact, Spanner, I can tell you I *know* we're talking about two different matters entirely, on my mother's—"

"You saying so doesn't make it a fact, Benny."

"Listen," Orkin squirms in the chair. "You got to understand I don't know for a fact where that broad is or where Vinton is at this time right here and now. But I think I can positively come by that information, you give me some time, don't tell anybody where I am, and pass me a bill now and then."

Orkin leans forward in the chair and points a finger. "What I can tell you for an abso-fucking-lutely fact is, I—number one—was never in nowhere with nobody with that drug shit. And for a number-two fact, neither was Vinton or the broad. The drugs was strictly a one-man operation, and the one man was Janish—"

The phone rings. It's sitting on the floor over by the bed. Benny stiffens in the chair as if he's suddenly stricken by paralysis. He stares at the phone hypnotically. The sweat pops out on his face. The phone rings again.

"You going to answer it, Benny? Or do you want me to do it?"

"Christ no, don't you answer it!" He's up out of the chair and rushes over to the phone. Before he picks it up, he says in a loud whisper, "Listen, Spanner, don't even breathe hard. If it's who I think it maybe is, you can blow the whole thing we been discussing."

As the phone rings for the third time, he snatches it up, sits on the edge of the bed, and says, "Yeah, hello . . . huh? I was in the crapper was why . . . Yeah . . . *yeah,* I said. Who you think would be here? . . . Oh, her, she's gone out . . . What? What the fuck is this, Twenty Questions? I sound strange, it's because I'm going stir-crazy is all . . ."

Orkin listens, biting his lip, and wiping the sweat off his face with his free hand. Then he says, "All I know is what I hear on the radio this morning . . . How they going to ask me anything, they don't know where I am? . . . My advice is yes, you're asking me, and the sooner the better is what I think . . . We're still talking the same deal, right? . . . Uh-huh, I got it. Right . . . *Come on, come on,* what's all this 'sound strange' shit? You're maybe getting a little stir-crazy yourself, is what I think . . . Yeah, I told you I got it, I got it . . . Same to you . . ."

Orkin hangs up the phone and puts it back on the floor. He lifts a corner of the bedsheet and wipes his dripping face before he turns and says, "That was the party I been waiting to hear from, Spanner. I think give me another couple of days, and it just may be I'll have some of that information you want."

"The party who called, Benny, would it be a name I know?"

"Like who?"

"Like Duane Vinton?"

"Vinton hisself, you mean?" His eyebrows go up. "Jesus, no, man! This is just a party's going to maybe give me some *information* on Vinton—"

"Uh-huh. Let it ride, Benny. Just as long as you understand one thing."

"What's that?"

"That's if I get my head chopped off by the cops because of you, I'm coming looking for you. And you know I'll find you. And you know what I'm going to do?"

Orkin blinks his eyes a couple of times. "What's that?"

"I'm going to hurt you, Benny. Bad. Hurt you so you'll wish I'd killed you instead. Do you understand?"

Orkin nods his head.

"Say it, Benny. Do you understand?"

"I understand."

"All right. Now, I want to use your phone, call my office."

"Sure, sure thing," he says eagerly, moving away from the bed. "Help yourself. Hey, how about I fix you a vodka and something?"

"No, thanks again just the same, Benny. It's going to be a long day."

"Listen," Orkin says, "you want me to duck into the can so's you can talk private?"

"No, it's all right. Fix yourself a drink. Relax."

The phone's ringing at the other end of the line. Lee answers. "J. T. Spanner's—"

"It's me, Lee, honey."

"J. T.! Are you all right?"

"I'm fine, yep."

"We were worried about you," Lee says. "All that stuff about you on the radio and in the newspapers—"

"I'm okay. Look, I'm out on the case right now. What's going on back there?"

"John Macauley called. He wanted to know if you needed any legal help."

"Call him back and tell him I'm in no trouble for the moment and that I'll talk to him later. What else?"

"Mrs. Balfe called. She says she's had a note from her daughter. She wants you to call her right away. And she wants you to see the note."

"Give me the phone number."

"It's nine-nine-nine-two-one-two-one."

"Got it."

"And, J. T.," Lee says, "I reached that U.S.-G. pilot, Joseph Shanley, you wanted to talk to. He can see you at three P.M. today at his apartment, if you're free. I'm supposed to call him back to verify."

"Call him. Tell him I'll be there. What's his address?"

There's the sound of some papers rustling and then she says, "It's Eleven Central Park West, right above Columbus Circle, The Park Eleven Apartments, the building's called. He said ask the doorman for him."

"I have it. Three o'clock."

"Also, J. T., I just spoke with Ellie. She's at her place. We both worked yesterday and last night typing up that stuff you wanted. Ellie just told me it's all done."

"Great. I want to see it. After I phone Mrs. Balfe and go up to the Bronx, I'll go down to Ellie's. Tell Ellie to stay there."

"Oh, and J. T., something else: you've gotten another of those calls where the party won't leave a name. This time it's a woman, a voice I haven't heard before. She's called three times."

"In that case, give me about two hours. Then give her the phone number at Ellie's. Is that it?"

"That's it."

Maybe it won't hurt Benny Orkin to overhear one side of the conversation with Margaret Balfe.

"I have to make one more call, Benny."

"Sure," he says, waving a hand in the air expansively.

Dial 999-2121.

"I'm calling Jill Balfe's mother, Benny. It should only take a second."

"Her, huh? It's all right." He's fixing himself a vodka.

Margaret Balfe picks up the phone on the second ring.

"Mrs. Balfe? This is J. T. Spanner."

"Oh, hello, Mr. Spanner. My goodness, I heard some news about you. I was terribly concerned. Does it have anything to do with my daughter?"

"Ah, no, ma'am, not that I know of. It was just one of those things out of left field—"

"You'll still be able to work on my daughter's case, won't you?" she asks anxiously.

"Oh, yes, ma'am. In fact, I'm working on it right now. I still don't have any solid information yet, but I did want to call you and let you know it's possible I may have something to report to you in another couple of days, unless I'm being misled in my investigation."

Across the room, Benny takes a fast gulp of his drink.

"It would be so nice if you did have something to tell me," Mrs. Balfe says wistfully. Her voice brightens as she says: "Oh, the reason I called you is I've had a note from Jill. I want you to see it."

"You're sure it's from her?"

"Yes, I'm sure. You can tell it for yourself when you compare the handwriting with other letters from her that I've kept. That's why I'd like you to see the note."

"I want to see it. I'll be up there within the hour. Goodbye now."

Benny clears his throat and, holding up his glass, says: "Sure you won't have one?"

"Thanks, no. I got to shove. You know something, Benny?"

"Huh, what?" He gets up to unlock the door.

"We're going to get some answers for the woman, Jill's mother. You and I. You know why I'm so sure?"

"Why's that?"

"Because like you always say, I swear it on my mother's grave. You understand?"

146

BRING BACK THE DEATH PENALTY

———Bumper sticker on car parked on West 259th Street

NOTHING'S changed in the house except Margaret Balfe's caftan. The one she's wearing today is a black-and-white print. Like the striped one she had on the day before yesterday, it, too, is damp with perspiration and there are, again, beads of perspiration along the hairline of her pinned-up black-black hair. The window shades are still drawn in the sitting room in the back of the house, and it looks as if another inch of dust has collected on the drooping plants in the past twenty-four hours.

The old woman—the mother-in-law—is sitting in a rocker in front of one of the TV sets which is tuned to some kind of game show, but the sound is turned down. Despite the heat, the old woman is wrapped up like a mummy in a red-and-blue wool afghan. Her eyes are closed.

"We can talk," Margaret Balfe says. She makes a motion toward her mother-in-law. "We won't disturb her. She's asleep, and anyway, she can't hear too well." Margaret Balfe leans forward, peering intently. "You're really all right, are you, Mr. Spanner? I mean, you didn't get hurt last night?"

"No. I came through unscathed. You mustn't worry yourself about me."

"I know. I know." Her head nods. "I expect you're able to take care of yourself, all right." She plucks nervously at the sofa's corduroy covering, that tremulous smile coming and going on her face.

"Mrs. Balfe, about the note—the note from Jill?"

"Oh, my, yes." She fumbles around in the folds of the caftan and holds out a white sheet of paper.

The note is written in pencil:

Dear Mama:

I know you are worried about me. But everything will be all right when we're together again. I pray I will be home soon. I miss you and Grandmama, too.

Love,
Your Jill

The handwriting is firm, each letter formed strong and clear.

"And you're sure this is Jill's handwriting?"

"You can see for yourself," she says and holds out a couple of more sheets of paper. "There are two letters Jill wrote me in the last few months."

One of the letters reads:

Dear Mama:

England is beautiful. We had a smooth flight. I am well and I hope you and Grandmama are, too. I won't get a chance to go to Ireland this trip. But I am seeing the sights. I will tell you all about it when I get home this weekend.

Love,
Your Jill

P.S. I bought you a present. I won't tell you what it is, but you can wear it to church.

The other letter is written on U.S.-G. Airlines stationery:

Dear Mama:

I can't believe I'm actually here in Rome! The Vatican looks just as I always pictured it would. I wish you were here with me. I'm still hoping to catch a glimpse of the Pope before I leave. It's all so exciting I'll have lots to tell you. Give Grandmama a kiss for me.

Love,
Your Jill

P.S. My cold is gone and I'm feeling fine.
P.P.S. The movie director, John Huston, was on the flight over! And guess what? I got his autograph! He's a nice man.

"You see, Mr. Spanner," Margaret Balfe says, "it's the same handwriting in all three letters."
"Well, I'm no expert on the subject but it sure looks the same. And the language sounds the same."
Mrs. Balfe sighs and plops back against the sofa cushions. "Oh, I was hoping you'd say that. I just knew the note was really from her."

"Still, the note doesn't tell us anything about where she is. What about the envelope? Where was it postmarked from?"

Her face goes blank. "What envelope?"

"The envelope the note came in."

"But there was no envelope, Mr. Spanner." She looks distressed. She holds up the note. "There was just this."

"Just that? Well, how did you get the note? I mean if it didn't come through the mail—?"

Mrs. Balfe is biting her lips. "I thought you understood. Jill dictated the note—"

"Dictated it? I don't get what you mean—oh, wait, now I think I understand. What you're trying to tell me is Jill dictated the note through the old—through your mother-in-law. That it?"

"Through Ardell, actually. You remember, Mother Balfe's spiritual guide—"

"Of course. Of course."

Jesus, Spanner, you bit again. Sonofabitch!

Mrs. Balfe's hands flutter in the air. "But there can't be any question about the handwriting, you said it yourself. Oh, this is from Jill, all right."

"Yes, of course, Mrs. Balfe."

She smiles contentedly and runs her fingers lovingly over the note. "I know you're probably working with the police in looking for Jill," she says. "So I'll let you use your judgment on whether to tell them about the note or not."

"I—ah—yes. I want to think about it."

She stirs herself on the sofa. "I don't want to keep you. I'm sure you're busy."

"That I am, Mrs. Balfe."

"I'll show you out. And thank you again for coming here today." She moves on toward the door to the hall.

In the rocking chair, the old woman's eyelids flicker, one eye shows piercingly for an instant, and the eyelids close quickly; she's been faking sleep, too.

> JOE (NO OTHER IDENT.): "—strangest goddamn thing I ever heard of, Karen. Why would she (UNINTELLIGIBLE)"
> KAREN: Beats me, Joe. Do you suppose she could have suffered amnesia . . .?"
>
> ——*transcript of tape recording originally labeled Apt. 4J, 600 E. 38th St. (#25)*

THERE are twenty-six tapes in all. Ellie has them stacked up alongside the recorder on the table in the dining alcove of her apartment. The tapes have been coded to correspond to the transcripts which Ellie and Lee have typed and which are also on the table.

"Can you make heads or tails out of our typing?" Ellie asks, coming out of the kitchen carrying a tray with a coffee service and two cups and saucers on it. "We couldn't figure out what some of the words on the tape were."

"The transcripts are fine for my purpose, honey. I'm just skimming through them to pick out the particular tapes I want to listen to."

Ellie sits down at the table and pours coffee into the cups. "You sure you don't want something to eat, J. T.?"

"No, just the coffee, thanks."

"I wish I'd had a little more warning you were coming so I could have straightened up the apartment better. But after Lee called and said you were on the way, all I had time to do was take a bath and get dressed—hurriedly, as you can see."

She's wearing a short blue denim skirt, a white halter tied at the midriff, and sandals.

"You look perfectly swell, Ellie, and so does the place."

Her apartment is on the seventh floor of a fourteen-story building on lower Fifth Avenue just a few paces from the Washington Square Arch.

The apartment consists of a small living room with an alcove for a table and two chairs, small bedroom, kitchen and bath, the whole place of about a size that would fit into the reception room of The Good Health Spa with space left over. The furniture is French Provincial, the carpeting a russet nylon pile, and the walls and ceilings a dark cream color, with ivory drapes at the windows. The place is as neat as a display in the furniture department of B. Altman's. But Ellie's always been a nut about neatness.

She takes a sip of her coffee and gets up. "You want me to put on the tapes you want to hear?" she asks.

"You're probably sick of listening to them by now. You don't have to hear them again unless you want to."

"I don't mind." She has that mischievous look on her face. "To tell you the truth, it's sort of fascinating to listen to them. Kind of like eavesdropping. Isn't that awful? Besides, you know you've never been any good at fooling around with mechanical things, and I've become an expert at working the tape recorder. Which tape do you want to hear first?"

"How about Number Fourteen? That's the one where the two girls leave the apartment, and later on there's the sound of somebody coming in there and moving around. Harry Flescher mentioned that tape to me. And can you skip the part where the two girls are talking before they go out and pick it up where it sounds like somebody's come in and is searching the place?"

"Number Fourteen coming up." Ellie picks the reel of

tape up from the stack, threads it into the recorder, and runs it at fast-forward motion. The dialogue between Bobbie and Karen sounds like the gibberish of cartoon characters on a speeded-up film. Then there's a long stretch of dead air. Finally, when the tape hits some barely audible sound, Ellie stops the machine, rewinds a section of tape, and presses the playback button.

There's a brief whirr of blank tape and then there's a faint sound of a click—door opening? . . . a click—door closing? . . . nothing . . . nothing . . . the sound, in the distance, of a door being shut . . . nothing . . . nothing . . . nothing . . . the sound, in the distance, of a door being shut . . . nothing . . . nothing . . . soft, tuneless whistling . . . tuneless whistling louder . . . the sound of drawers being opened and closed . . . tuneless whistling louder . . . soft breathing . . . tuneless whistling recedes . . . very faint the sound of drawers being opened and closed . . . tuneless whistling . . . the sound of a phone ringing shrilly . . . the whistling stops . . . the phone rings nine times . . . the phone stops ringing . . . the tuneless whistling resumes . . . recedes . . . there's the faint sound of a click—door opening? . . . a click—door closing? . . . nothing . . . nothing . . . nothing . . .

"That's all there is on the rest of that tape," Ellie says. "I listened to the end when I typed it up."

"There was sure as hell somebody in there, all right."

Ellie nods. "I didn't know what was on the tape before I listened to it while I was transcribing it. I actually got goose pimples when I came to that part."

"Tell me, honey, did you get any impression—any feeling about that unseen person while you were listening?"

Ellie frowns. "Just that, well, I'd say it was a man. Don't ask me why. But it's just the way I feel."

"That's interesting. Harry Flescher had the same feeling. And so do I."

The phone rings. Ellie answers it, then says, "J. T., Lee just got a call from that Mrs. Balfe. Mrs. Balfe wants to talk to you. Says her mother-in-law got some kind of message about Jill. That Jill was going to call them. And then they got a phone call and whoever called hung up. Mrs. Balfe wants to know if you think it was Jill."

"Oh, Jesus! Those crazy old women! Somebody calls a wrong number and they get into a flap. I need all this crap like I need a hole in the head. Tell Lee to tell her to go to—No, no, just tell Lee to tell Mrs. Balfe to keep in touch. That I don't think the call was important, but I'll call her later."

Ellie comes back over. "What do you want to hear next?"

"Let's try tape Number Six. According to the transcript, that's where the two girls are discussing Jill Balfe's disappearance right after the police have been there to question them about it. I want to hear how their voices sound when they're alone talking to each other about the case."

Ellie puts the new tape on the recorder:

SOUND: Ice tinkling in a glass.
KAREN: Well, kid, here's to our missing roomie.
BOBBIE: That's not very funny, Karen. Something serious could have happened to her.
KAREN: Oh, I don't mean it that way, love. I liked Jill well enough. Square Jill. What I don't like is all the fuzz flatfooting it in and out of here.
BOBBIE: What do you really think happened to her?
KAREN: Maybe she got carried off in a flying saucer from outer space.
BOBBIE: Come on, Karen, be serious.
KAREN: Why be serious? What I *hope* happened is that she's off somewhere fucking her brains out. Be the best thing that ever happened to her.
BOBBIE: But she didn't have to disappear to do that. She's got a bedroom right through that door there.
KAREN: Passion, it could have been passion. 'Swept

away on a blah, blah, blah, blah'—whatever the hell the name of that movie was, the Italian one.

BOBBIE: But you don't *really* think that's what happened to her.

KAREN: No, Barbara Ann, I guess I really don't. The truth is, I guess I really think she could be—dead, which is what I think the police suspect. Only, I don't want to think that.

BOBBIE: But why would anyone kill her?

KAREN: Jesus, how would I know? Maybe some rapist grabbed her, some pervert. Maybe she was kidnapped. Maybe—oh, I don't know—maybe anything. What I do know is all this talk is morbid. I'll have nightmares all night. I'm going to fix myself another drink. A good, stiff one. Look, maybe she just wanted to get away for a while by herself, so she up and left.

BOBBIE: I wish we knew something. This—

Bobbie's next words are unintelligible, and the tape ends there.

Ellie rewinds the reel. "What do you think, J. T.?" she asks. "Did you catch anything in their voices?"

"It's hard to say. They both sounded natural enough, as far as I could tell. If there's something one or the other knows and hasn't told, it would appear they don't *both* know it, that they aren't in collusion. Of course, either of them could be trying to fake out the other."

Ellie nods. "That Karen, particularly, is a character, you know. There's some stuff in there that has nothing to do with your case but is pretty titillating—Karen with a whole succession of men. It gets hot and heavy. We'd make a fortune if we could market those sections and title them 'Tapes to Get Turned On By.' "

"Yeah, well, maybe I'll get around to hearing them later. I'm going to have to be leaving soon for an appointment with that pilot, Joe Shanley. But at least now, after reading all the transcripts, I know what's on the tapes, even if they didn't really tell me anything new about where Jill Balfe is, or who knows what about her disappearance."

"How about some more coffee," Ellie says. Before she can pour the coffee, the phone rings.

"That must be Lee," Ellie says and goes over, picks up the phone and says, "Hello," and then, "Yes, he's here. May I ask who's calling?" She covers the phone with her hand and holds it out. "It's for you, J. T." In a whisper, she adds, "It's a woman. She says she called your office, and was told to call you here. She wouldn't give her name; she said you didn't know her."

"Okay, I'll take it."

Ellie goes back to the table.

"Hello, this is J. T. Spanner."

"Mr. Spanner." The woman's voice at the other end of the line is husky, assured. "You don't know me. My name is Julia Angstrom. I think I'm in need of your services. I wonder if it would be possible for you to meet with me this evening, say about eight P.M.? At my apartment."

"Could you give me some idea of the nature of your problem?"

"I'd prefer not, until we've met. However, I will tell you that it won't take up much of your time, and that the fee will be generous. Yes or no?"

"Yes, all right. We'll talk. What's your address?"

"It's 642 Park Avenue," she says. "That's between Sixty-sixth and Sixty-seventh Street, Apartment 12K. I'll expect you promptly at eight." She hangs up.

Ellie looks up from stirring her coffee. "Who was *she?*"

"Somebody named Julia Angstrom. A rich somebody, apparently. Park Avenue, no less. She wants to hire me for a job, and she says it won't take up much of my time and the fee will be generous."

"Ho! Ho! Ho!" Ellie laughs. "You know what *that* sounds like. Speaking of which, I heard that Bobbie Gillian on the tapes making a play for you when you went to her apartment to talk about Jill Balfe. Let me tell you something, J. T."

"What's that?"

"You stay away from that Bobbie doll, 'cause I've got news for you."

"Yeah, what?"

"If she hooks you, you get married again, and you divorce her—as you would—there's not enough business in the office for *three* of us."

> CIVILIAN
> Radio Taxi
> Patrol
> Direct Contact with
> Your Police Dept.
> Sponsored by
> CitiBank
>
> ——*Decal shield on right front fender of Cab
> No. 5T 77579S*

THERE was a time, not too long ago, when only a handful of apartment buildings in Manhattan had names—like The Dakota, The Osborne, The River House—but then, recently, every place they put up, they gave a fancy name. The name of some famous painter or public figure or a name the owners and renting agents probably hoped would sound impressive—like The Eureka, The Pinnacle, The Something-Plaza, The Plaza-Something, The Park-Something, The Water-Something. But just try giving a New York City cab driver one of the new-minted names, and you get a blank stare in return. They know from nothing about apartment house names, except maybe for The Dakota, The Osborne, The River House.

The building where the pilot, Joe Shanley, lives—known to God-knows-who, but certainly not cab drivers, as The Park Eleven Apartments—is a posh, *West Side* forty-one floor high rise.

The doorman is tall, silver-haired, uniformed, white

gloved, outwardly one of your Mr. Affable types while the rest of him remains distantly remote behind pink-tinted eyeglasses.

"Oh, yes, Mr. Spanner," he says with a fake glad-to-see-you smile, "Mr. Shanley left word he was expecting you. He asked that you join him at The Sun Deck Club on the roof. Just take the elevator on your left to the forty-first floor."

The elevator is an automatic, express, with piped-in music, which whisks upwards in something like twenty-one seconds and the doors open and you're there, feeling as though your socks and shorts are still forty-one floors down below.

The Sun Deck Club is quite a setup. The elevator doors open directly into a glassed-in bar and lounge overlooking an outdoor pool and sun deck and, beyond the parapets of the roof, the skyline of Manhattan. There are people sitting around the bar and at some of the tables. The place is like a nifty sky-high nightclub, air-conditioned cool and with more piped-in music in the background.

Sliding glass doors lead out to the pool area where there are chaises and deck chairs. There are maybe thirty people lounging around the pool, or in the water, most of them pulchritudinous females, more than not in string bikinis.

One of the few males in view, a dark-haired guy in madras swim trunks stretched out on a rubber float near the pool, waves a hand lazily in the air and calls out, "Hey, you Spanner? Come on over." There's a blonde in a pink bikini sitting next to him on the float, smoothing suntan lotion over her long legs.

The guy pushes himself up effortlessly from the float, stands, and sticks out his hand. "I figured you had to be Spanner. You got that cop look. I'm Joe Shanley."

"I appreciate your seeing me."

"Not at all. Not at all," he says.

Shanley's about six feet tall, weighs about 170 pounds, is in his late thirties, and has the look of the Black Irish:

hair the color of coal oil, and on his chest, arms, and legs, too, dark eyes, dusky skin, and a rough-hewn face.

"How about we have a drink while we talk?" Shanley asks. "What would you like?"

"A beer'll be okay. Let me buy."

Shanley waves a hand. "No. I have to sign a tab for it." He turns and says to the blonde, "Hey, Daphne, how about you get Mr. Spanner and me a drink, huh? He'll have a beer, and I'll take another bloody mary."

The blonde gets up and Shanley gives her a light pat on her bottom before she trots away toward the bar.

"Hell of a beautiful day, huh?" Shanley says, lifting his face to the sun.

The overcast of early morning has burned away, and the sky is a clear blue from horizon to horizon. The dry wind that puffs across the rooftop from the west now and then is like a spurt from a hot-air blow-dryer.

"Yeah, it is. This is a nice place you got up here."

"That it is," Shanley agrees. "Beats the city's public baths all to hell." He laughs.

The blonde—Daphne—comes back with the drinks.

"Thanks, Daff," Shanley says. "You be a good girl now and soak up some sun while Mr. Spanner and I take a walk and do some talking." He reaches down and picks up a pair of binoculars by the leather straps. "Come on Spanner."

He heads over to the far side of the roof, saying, "We'll have a little more privacy over here."

At the west edge of the roof, Shanley sets the binocular on a waist-high stone ledge and takes a sip of his bloody mary.

The view from the spot is slightly dizzying. To the north, south, east, and west, the top floors of the surrounding buildings look so close—even as far south as the Empire State Building on 34th Street, as far east as the United Nations Building on the East River, as far west as the apartment-house complexes on the Jersey Palisades across the Hudson River, as far north as the taller housing projects in Harlem—that you feel you could reach out and touch them. And, surprisingly, from up here, you can spot swimming pools on the rooftops of countless apartment buildings all over the city. It's like discovering the existence of another world that's totally hidden from the people plodding and sweating on the streets far below. Not many blocks to the west, the sun is sparkling on the dark blue waters of the Hudson where five or six ocean liners are berthed at the West Side docks. Jutting out in the river, to the northwest, is the 79th Street Marina where Duane Vinton has his houseboat. There are several barges and tankers and small boats moving along the river and a police helicopter, patrolling the Hudson, appears in the sky to the north and comes skimming over the water downriver. Higher up and farther away, to the southwest, a couple of silver-colored jetliners are headed out over the Atlantic.

Shanley takes a look at the jetliners through his binoculars and says: "A Pan Am and a British Airways."

He puts the binoculars back on the ledge, takes another sip of his drink, and says, "About Jill Balfe, Spanner, what can I do for you?"

"Well, I understand you were one of the last persons who saw her at JFK the night she disappeared—"

"Yeah, so the police informed me."

"—and I wanted to talk to you about that, among other things."

Shanley nods. "Uh-huh. Well, to go back to that night, I saw Jill right after we cleared customs. We spoke for no more than a moment. Making conversation. I asked her if she was tired. She said no, it had been an easy flight, no hassling. I said maybe I'd be seeing her around at a party, and she said, 'Sure.' And that was it, nothing. I walked on to the U.S.-G. Building. The last I saw of her, she was talking to a Pan Am stewardess we both know, Jenny Cupperton."

"And she—Jill—appeared okay to you? I mean, like nothing was troubling her?"

"Nothing I could detect at the time, and even now looking back on it."

"All right, now let's talk about your personal impressions of Jill in the time you've known her. I understand you saw her socially on some occasions."

"I did," Shanley says, "but I wasn't romancing her, anything like that, you know."

"I realize that, from what I've heard. I'm not suggesting anything. We're just talking. I'd like to find out what happened to her. I'm assuming you want to help me."

Shanley takes a sip of his drink. "Hell, yes, I do. I never had any strong feelings about her one way or the other, but I thought she was a good kid. If she got into any serious trouble or if anybody did anything to harm her, I want to help."

"That's why I'd like you to give me your impressions of her."

"Since she came to work for U.S.-G.," Shanley says, "she was part of my crew for oh, maybe twenty, twenty five flights. She was always easy to get along with. She was a quick learner. As I guess you've found out by now she'd apparently had a pretty sheltered life before she moved away from home. That was fairly obvious when she first came to work for us. But she also had a kind of eagerness about her which was appealing. Like she was anxious to have all the experiences she'd never had before."

"Would that include sexual experiences, too, would you say?"

Shanley hesitates for a moment before he says, "First hand, I wouldn't know. But my impression would be yes. Look, let me say something candidly, and I have to hope you won't misunderstand and think I'm a *macho* horse's ass."

"Try me."

"First, let me say those scurrilous tales that everybody's heard at one time or another about pilots and stewardesses screwing in the cabin while the plane's flying on automatic at fifty thousand feet, or whatever, simply *ain't* true. Believe me."

"I believe you."

"However"—he says and pauses and cocks his head to one side, an amused, mocking look on his face—"however, it *is* true that a pilot—and because he's a pilot—who is single, as I am, doesn't lead an exactly monastic life."

"Yeah?"

"So what I'm saying," Shanley says, "is after a while a guy like me develops an ability—an instinct—before he tries to score, to figure out whether a gal wants to get laid or doesn't, and whether she's going to let you go afterwards, or she's going to cling to you. In my judgment, Jill Balfe fitted the first category and the last. I never made it with her, never tried to."

"But somebody else might have, huh?"

Shanley nods. "It's possible."

"Let's talk about something else. Tell me about when you go through customs, after a flight, exactly what happens there, how thoroughly do they go over you?"

The question seems to puzzle Shanley, and he's thinking about it as he answers, "At Kennedy, you talking about?"

"At Kennedy."

"Let's see. Well, for one thing, we—the flight crews—go through a separate customs examination from the passengers. But you probably already knew that. As far as how thoroughly they examine you is concerned, it varies."

"Varies how?"

Shanley sets his drink on the ledge and spreads the fingers of his right hand in the air. "I mean, sometimes they just ask you if you have anything to declare and if you say no, they pass you right through. Another time, they might shake down your luggage. Still other times, they might do the whole bit: search the luggage, your clothes, make you strip, and *then* probe your body like you're taking a physical."

"And you never know from one time to the next what kind of search it's going to be?"

Shanley shakes his head. "Nope. I figure that's why they vary the routine, to keep you guessing, so you're afraid to try to get away with anything."

Shanley squints into the sun for a minute, then picks up his glass and finishes off his bloody mary. "You know," he says, "now I have to ask you something."

"Yeah?"

"We're having a conversation about Jill Balfe and all of a sudden you're questioning me about how does customs handle airlines personnel. Well, that's got to make me curious. Are you suggesting she might have been involved in smuggling?"

"Let me put it to you this way: it's one of those questions I have to ask since, after all, there have been such cases involving stewardesses. I've heard of them and so have you, I imagine."

"Yeah, I know it's happened," Shanley agrees. "Drugs usually. But knowing the way customs works, as she did, Jill'd have to be damn stupid to risk it."

"Probably she didn't. Like I said, it's just one of those questions you have to ask. Look, I thank you for talking with me. I'm going to leave you one of my cards. If you recall anything else about Jill, I'd sure like to hear."

"Will do," Shanley says. "And I hope you find her." He frowns and adds, "I don't envy you the job. While we've been talking, I've been looking down at the city there and wondering, Jesus, with all the places there are to look, how would you ever find anybody? It's like a concrete anthill."

> . . . There are 560 miles of sewers and 50 underground streams beneath the streets of Manhattan. On Park Avenue, the New York Central Railroad tracks run beneath the street and all the structures on the avenue are built on steel and concrete stilts between the tracks below. Park Avenue's asphalt crust is only four inches thick in spots, which makes it the thinnest layer of street surface in all of Manhattan . . .

THE living room of Julia Angstrom's Park Avenue apartment looks as though it was furnished by Thomas Chippendale's decorator—which is the period style of the sofa, settee, and chairs, all of them covered in mauve satin. There are drapes of the same color and material, hung from a brass traverse rod that encircles the room near the ceiling of what could be the second floor if they ever decided to build a duplex apartment inside the room. The drapes are now open so you can see that the walls on three sides of the room are lined by bronze-framed mirrors. The fourth wall is a series of latticed windows that resemble French doors and overlook Park Avenue. There are no rugs on the floor, which is dark marble, and from the center of the ceiling hangs a multitiered crystal chandelier lit up like the Rockefeller Center Christmas tree on December 24.

The maid who has answered the door to the apartment,

led the way to the living room, and said, "Please wait here. Miz Angstrom'll be right down," has disappeared.

Some minutes pass until precisely, with the sound of a clock somewhere in the apartment chiming the hour of 8:00 P.M., a woman comes through the doorway.

"Mr. Spanner," she says, hand outstretched, "I'm Julia Angstrom."

She's a handsome woman who must be in her late forties, early fifties, with the kind of firm body and smooth, creamy skin that shows a lot of time, money, and attention must have been lavished on them. Her hair is dark blonde with light blonde streaks highlighting it in spots. She has an ample bosom which noticeably fills out the top of her jade silk dress, good legs sheathed in the sheerest nylons, and her shoes are black patent-leather pumps. She's wearing a thin gold band around her throat, tiny gold earrings, and some kind of delicate sandalwood perfume.

Julia Angstrom points at the Chippendale sofa and says, "Sit there, Mr. Spanner."

She takes a seat in the armchair next to the sofa. "Now," she says, "my first question is, why were you so hesitant when I spoke to you on the phone and asked if you could see me?"

"That was before you told me the job you wanted me for wouldn't take much time. I'm in the middle of another case at the moment and, ethically, I didn't feel I could divide any time between my other client and you."

She nods. "Another question: of course I read in the papers about the shooting you were involved in last night. Are you going to have trouble with the police because of it?"

"I have no reason to think so, no. I gave them a statement. It was self-defense. But if that bothers you perhaps you'd better get someone else—"

"No, no, no," she says, "I want you. Good Lord, don' be so prickly, Mr. Spanner. It was, wasn't it, a perfectly logical question to ask?"

"Yes, of course. It was a logical question. And now that we've got all that out of the way, suppose you tell me what it is you want to hire me for?"

"I will," she says, "but first I have to know if you're willing to do something for me?"

"Yeah, what's that?"

"Would you," she asks, "permit me to search you so I can be certain you're not carrying any electronics equipment on your person?"

"You mean you think I might be wearing a wire—? That's a new one. No, I don't mind, go ahead. Who knows, I might even enjoy it."

Julia Angstrom doesn't smile. She comes over. Her hands move and pat, impersonally, expertly, up, down, in, out and under, coat, shirt, and trousers.

When she's finished, she goes back to her chair and sits down.

"Satisfied?"

She nods.

"You know, Mrs. Angstrom, you'd make a good cop."

"I don't know whether I should take that as a compliment or not," she says.

"Okay, can we get on with what you want to hire me for?"

Julia Angstrom sits very still, her eyes fixed on the windows as she talks. "Tomorrow I have a—ah—business meeting with someone. There will be money exchanged, from me to this person, quite a large sum of money. I'd like you to accompany me to the meeting."

"This large sum of money, how much is it?"

She doesn't answer. Instead, she gets up from the chair and goes over to one of the bronze-framed mirrors on the wall. She does something at the side of the frame, and the mirrored panel swings out. Behind it is a wall safe. She twists the dials on the safe door, opens it, and lifts out a cowhide attaché case.

She brings the attaché case back, places it on the sofa,

and lifts the lid. The inside is filled with neatly stacked packs of thousand-dollar bills.

"Jesus! How much is in there?"

"Two hundred and fifty thousand dollars, Mr. Spanner," she says.

"Two hundred—Are you crazy? Why would you trust me enough to show me that kind of cash? You've never seen me before tonight. How do you know I won't knock you in the head and walk off with it? Lady, you don't need a private detective, you need a keeper."

Julia Angstrom settles back in her chair and for the first time she laughs, a deep, throaty laugh. "Oh, I know all about you, Mr. Spanner. In fact, I have a complete dossier on you. Yes, I think I can trust you."

"Where would you get a complete dossier on me?"

She laughs again. She's enjoying herself. "Why, from a private detective, of course."

"You mean you hired a private detective to check me out before you tried to hire me—? Oh, hold it! I get it now; you mean Harry Flescher? He worked for you?"

Julia Angstrom sits up on the edge of the chair. "That's right, Mr. Spanner. Harry Flescher. I was his employer at the time he was killed. Of course, I didn't hire him to check you out. But he told me about meeting you the night before he was killed. By the time he talked to me, he'd run a complete check on you from whatever sources he used, and he told me a considerable amount about you, professionally and personally. From what he told me, I feel I can trust you."

"What you really hired him for, was it to look for Duane Vinton?"

"To find Duane Vinton, yes," she says. "That interests you, doesn't it, because of the girl you're looking for? Harry Flescher told me you were looking for the girl. When he—Flescher—was killed, I decided, when the time was right, to try to hire you to replace him. Because of this meeting tomorrow, which I only found out about today, I need your services."

"Just to protect the money?"

"Perhaps more than that." She pauses and then adds, "There could be some complications."

"Mrs.—incidentally, what is it—Mrs. or what?"

She nods. "Mrs. But I've been a widow for—oh, a great many years now."

"Mrs. Angstrom, don't you think the time has come when you'd better tell me the whole story—that is, if you want to retain my services."

Julia Angstrom runs a finger nervously around the inside of the gold band that encircles her throat. "Yes. I suppose I'll have to. But I want you to understand, Mr. Spanner, if you ever tell anyone else—including the police—the story I'm about to tell you, I'll deny it and there's no way anyone can prove it. I never even told Harry Flescher any of this."

"Yeah. Well, go on."

"To begin at the beginning," she says, "I've known Duane Vinton for about a year. I was for a time a member of that health spa where he worked and we became—became very close—friends. He seemed to know his way around, and there's a certain form of business which he's been able to take care of for me. I had grown to trust him—"

"This business—it wouldn't by chance have involved smuggling, would it?"

Julia Angstrom's face goes deadly white, and there's a tremor in her voice when she whispers, "Smuggling? Where on earth did you get an idea like that?"

"Smuggling drugs, to be specific."

"Oh, dear heavens, Mr. Spanner"— the relief in her voice is evident—"you gave me a start for a moment! But oh, no, no, of course my business with Duane Vinton didn't involve smuggling drugs. Drugs!" She gives that throaty laugh again. "Look at me. Do I look like the kind of person who would be involved with smuggling drugs?"

"There's no answer to that, Mrs. Angstrom. All kinds of people are involved with drugs these days."

"Well, I'm not, I assure you." She smiles. "The most perfunctory investigation on your part would have revealed—will reveal—that I conduct a highly profitable business in rare gems. I have my own shop in the Diamond District on West Forty-seventh Street. I have a full staff to run the place. I specialize in dealing with private clients; procuring for them, whenever possible, the very rarest gems whenever such stones are available anywhere in the world."

"All right. I'll take your word for it. So, what does your business have to do with Duane Vinton?"

Julia Angstrom sighs softly. "Now we are approaching delicate ground, Mr. Spanner. I must choose my words carefully. Let me explain that the kind of clients with whom I do business are extremely reluctant to have it known when they purchase a rare gem, especially if it is a world-famous stone. They are persons of great wealth. They shun notoriety, and they're also fearful of gem thieves."

Julia Angstrom pauses as if searching for words before she continues. "I am known to diamond merchants all over the world, and many of the offerings I receive come from various dealers in foreign countries. Consequently the problem of maintaining secrecy in such transactions is most difficult when the gems have to be transported from for instance, Europe to the United States—"

"Because of customs—?"

"Well yes, among other—"

"So I was right. We are talking about smug—"

"*Please*, Mr. Spanner," she interrupts quickly. "You must not insert words into this conversation which I have not used. For your protection—legal protection—as well as mine. May I proceed?"

"Yeah, go ahead."

"When Duane and I became close friends, I happened to mention this particular—ah—problem. Not long afterward, he told me he thought he'd figured out a possible solution."

"Uh-huh. And you didn't ask him precisely what his solution was?"

Julia Angstrom smiles radiantly. "Exactly, Mr. Spanner, I did not. We simply agreed that he would act as an intermediary, for which he would be paid."

"Sort of like a messenger boy—is that it?"

"That's one way of putting it, yes." She nods. "As to what he planned to do, how he planned to do it, when he planned to do it, I know nothing of such things."

"And you think that by pleading ignorance of his methods—even if they happened to be illegal—you can stay out of jail, if it should ever come to that?"

"Jail, my goodness," she says as if she's never considered the possibility. "Why should I go to jail for simply entering into a business transaction? Besides, I think it *would* keep me out of jail, if it should ever come to that. Yes."

"Okay, so Duane Vinton solved your problem for you. So what happened?"

Julia Angstrom leans back in her chair. "For a time, everything worked splendidly. On perhaps half a dozen occasions during the past year, he delivered to me certain—ah—pieces which I had purchased elsewhere, and which I then sold to one or another of my clients in this country. The arrangement seemed ideal—until this last time." She shakes her head sadly. "This one time, I was indiscreet. My enthusiasm for this particular gem was so great, I was so excited, and I had grown to completely trust Duane."

She smiles sadly. "As has been said, Mr. Spanner, there's no fool like an *aging* fool—female, like me—when she's enthralled by a young male buck—like Duane Vin-

171

ton. Need I say more? Foolishly, I told him much more than I should have about the stone. If I hadn't, perhaps the arrangement would have continued without incident. Once he knew what he would have in his hand—well, I guess the temptation was too great for him to resist."

Julia Angstrom gets up from her chair. "Let me show you something." She walks toward a candlestand table where a thick leather-bound book is lying. "Have you ever heard of the Sancy Diamond, Mr. Spanner? How much do you know about diamonds?"

"Let me put it to you this way, Mrs. Angstrom: I know a bail bondsman named Hymie Rosen who wears a diamond pinkie ring. I've been told the stone is a certified multicarat blue-white gem. That's about the extent of my knowledge."

> From the form and cut of the stone, there can be no doubt but that the Sancy Diamond originated in India. Most historians trace this date from about 1570. The Sancy's "water" and brilliance are said to be the finest order. It is a 54-carat, almond-shaped gem . . .
>
> ——The Encyclopedia of Precious Gems
> *compiled by Sir James Moncrief, 1892*

"SIR James Moncrief is only one of several recognized authorities in the field who have over the years documented the rarity of the Sancy Diamond," Julia Angstrom says, taking the leather-bound book and placing it in the chair beside her. "I wanted you to see that the stone has been legitimately authenticated before I tell you its history."

"Yes, all right, I'm listening. I'm convinced of its authenticity."

"And I'm sure I don't have to tell you"—she makes a gesture with her hand—"that the value of the Sancy is almost impossible to calculate. Fifty-four carats, can you imagine?"

"No, I can't imagine. But if you say so, I believe you."

Julia Angstrom smiles politely, but she's anxious to tell her story, and she says quickly, "The existence of the diamond—the Sancy—first became known when it was brought to France by Nicolas Harlal, Duke de Sancy, who was the French ambassador to the Ottoman Court, about the year 1570. It's believed the duke purchased the stone in Constantinople in that year."

"Yeah, uh-huh."

"According to various histories"—she taps the book in the chair beside her—"the duke sold or loaned the diamond to Henry the Third, who was then king of France. It's said that the monarch used the Sancy Diamond as an ornament in the front of a cap which he wore on his head at all times because he was sensitive about being bald."

She shakes her head and smiles as she says, "And they talk about the vanity of women! In any event, in time the duke took possession of the diamond again. Somewhat later when Henry the Fourth succeeded to the throne, the duke was once more called upon to loan the fabulous gem. This time Henry the Fourth needed it to use as collateral to obtain money to hire soldiers for the French army. And now occurred one of the most incredible incidents in the incredible history of the Sancy Diamond."

Julia Angstrom pauses dramatically before she says, "On the night the duke's trusted courier was delivering the diamond to the king, thieves attacked the courier near the Louvre and killed him. Other servants of the duke's household found the dead courier lying in the street and brought the body home. The duke immediately searched the dead man's clothes, but couldn't find the diamond. The duke believed he was ruined since the diamond, although it was no larger in size than a peach pit, had brought him honors and high royal posts. Looking down upon the dead body of his trusted courier, the duke had a remarkable thought, Mr. Spanner. Do you know what it was?"

"Nope. Tell me."

Julia Angstrom squeezes her eyes shut. "He decided that the courier might have swallowed the diamond to protect it, and he slit the man's body open with a knife."

She opens her eyes. "And there it was—the diamond was recovered. It was loaned to the king, and he was able to use it to hire soldiers for the French army."

"That's a hell of a story, all right."

"Oh, that's not all." Julia Angstrom folds her hands together. "Eventually, the diamond was returned to the Duke de Sancy. Somewhere between 1590 and 1600, he sold it to Queen Elizabeth of England. It became one of the English crown jewels and remained in the collection until the widow of Charles the First, the Dowager Queen Henrietta Maria, presented it to Somerset, Earl of Worcester. From there it passed into the hands of King James the Second of England and from him to Louis the Fourteenth of France in about 1695. The diamond, along with the throne, was then inherited by Louis the Fifteenth. My God, Mr. Spanner, think of the history of which it's been a part!"

"Yeah, there's that, all right, Mrs. Angstrom."

"Yes." She nods dreamily. "Next, to continue, in 1792, there was the famous robbery of the Garde Meuble in Paris and the Sancy Diamond—along with the most famous of the French crown jewels—disappeared."

"Aha."

Julia Angstrom raises a hand. "I know what you're thinking, Mr. Spanner; that it's been missing since. But there's still a bit more of its known history yet. The Sancy Diamond reappeared in 1828, when it was sold by a respectable French dealer to a Russian prince. Then, in 1867, it was exhibited in the Paris Exposition and was said to be the property of a French firm. According to some accounts, the Sancy Diamond later returned to India, to Bombay. Some rumors have it that the diamond was bought there by a maharajah, and that it may or may not have changed hands many times since. And that whoever owned it would naturally want to keep the fact secret. But these are only rumors, Mr. Spanner, and the actual fact is that for all intents and purposes, the Sancy vanished over a century ago. And ever since then every diamond dealer has had his eye out for it."

"All right, I'm waiting for the punch line, Mrs. Angstrom."

"Yes, you've guessed it." Her eyes are shining. "I think the Sancy Diamond has been located again. And two months ago it was offered to me by a merchant in Europe with whom I have had dealings for many years. I have a buyer who will pay a fortune for it."

"Are you sure it's the genuine Sancy Diamond?"

"No. I won't know that positively until I've examined the stone for myself."

"This merchant—he doesn't happen to be located in Antwerp, Belgium, does he?"

"No, he doesn't. But"—she winks—"he was in Antwerp this week. At that time he notified me that the diamond had been picked up by someone who said they were representing me, and that it was on its way to me. I made a deposit in the Swiss account of this particular merchant—which is the way such transactions are handled."

"And the diamond?"

Julia Angstrom makes an empty-handed gesture in the air. "I'm still waiting for it to arrive. Today I received a phone call that I could have the diamond tomorrow in exchange for two hundred and fifty thousand dollars in cash."

"And the phone call came from Duane Vinton?"

Julia Angstrom moistens her lips with her tongue before she answers. "Mr. Spanner, I've told you a great many confidential facts about myself. I think the time has come when you have to tell me whether or not you're going to work for me. Before I tell you anything else." She adds quickly, "I'm prepared to pay you twenty-five thousand dollars if we are successful in getting the diamond. Yes or no?"

"Yes, Mrs. Angstrom. You just hired me."

She claps her hands together. "Good."

"Now, about the phone call—"

"Yes," she says quickly, "the phone call was from Duane Vinton. He says he has the diamond."

"Did he give you any explanation of why he hadn't contacted you before?"

"No." She shakes her head. "But I think I know why. I think Mr. Duane Vinton has been playing games with me."

"Games? What kind of games? Why?"

"To drive up his price, of course. You see, there are some things that have gone on which you don't know about."

"All right. Tell me."

"Well," Julia Angstrom sighs resignedly, "back at the time just before he disappeared and I couldn't find him, Duane did an unusual thing which meant nothing to me when it occurred. He came to me one day and said he was having trouble with his car and asked if he could borrow one of mine—"

"I'd guess you own a Toyota, right?"

"One of my cars is a Toyota, yes. He had it the night some girl's body was found on the Queensboro Bridge, and the story was in the newspapers about the body being stolen by some people driving a Toyota, and about an airline stewardess disappearing—the one, I believe, you're looking for. The next day, my car—the Toyota—was returned. It was left parked in the apartment-building garage where I keep my cars. But there was no sign of Duane. And I never heard from him again until the phone call today. You see?"

"No, frankly, Mrs. Angstrom, I'm afraid I don't see."

She shifts in the chair impatiently. "Don't you *see*, it was all stage-managed, a hoax. That should be clear. The *Toyota*—he knew I'd recognize that it was the car he'd borrowed from me as soon as I read the stories in the papers—"

177

"I'm sorry. I must be dense. I still don't see what you're driving at."

Julia Angstrom has a pained expression on her face. "Look, let me suggest what I think happened. Duane has the Sancy Diamond. He and the stewardess are in this thing together—but you understand I know nothing about her part—"

"You know nothing *legally,* you mean?"

She nods. "But say they're in it together and they've decided to keep the diamond and try to sell it on their own; or keep it for a while, so they can possibly drive up the price they want from me. So he disappears, thinking he'll stay hidden until he's disposed of it. But, believe me, it's not that easy to sell off a stone as valuable as the Sancy; so then finally, today, he calls me and offers it to me."

"I still don't follow you about the business of the stolen body, the Toyota—"

"Don't you see?" Julia Angstrom asks pleadingly. "If they planned to hide with the diamond for a while, to sell it to somebody else or to me, they had to find a way to keep me quiet; to make me think something had happened, and that's what all that business with the body being stolen was designed to do. And, possibly, to make me think it was the stewardess's body."

"You mean you think Duane Vinton and the stewardess, Jill Balfe, were the two individuals who held up the morgue wagon and stole the body of the unidentified girl?"

"Exactly, Mr. Spanner, exactly."

"But then, who was the unidentified dead girl? How did Vinton and Jill Balfe, the stewardess, know about her body?"

"I don't know who the dead girl was." She smiles wisely. "But I can tell you this: I use the Toyota for trips to the country, and there were several pairs of khaki coveralls in the car. The dead girl could have been anyone, and they heard about her while they were driving in from the airport; you see, Mr. Spanner, the Toyota is equipped with a radio that picks up police calls! They could have been planning something else and acted on the spur of the moment when they heard about the body."

"Mrs. Angstrom, your suggestion flabbergasts me."

"Well," she says, "there it is."

"I don't know. I don't know what to think. Tell me about tomorrow—what instructions did Vinton give you?"

"I'm to bring my money to that houseboat of his—you know about the houseboat?"

"Yes. At the Seventy-ninth Street Marina—"

"Yes. I'm to bring the money there at exactly four P.M. tomorrow afternoon." She lifts her hand palm up. "You will help me, won't you?"

"I tell you, Mrs. Angstrom, I wouldn't miss that meeting for all the diamonds I can think of—your Sancy, the Hope Diamond, the Kohinoor Diamond, and the one in the pinkie ring of Hymie Rosen, the bail bondsman."

Julia Angstrom laughs. "Mr. Spanner, you are an original."

> . . . Forecasters of the National Weather
> Service are 87% accurate in predicting rain
> for the same day, 80% for the next day, and
> in predicting temperatures are accurate
> within 3½° for average forecasting on the
> same day and the same night, within 4½°
> for the next day . . .

HEAVY rain has been falling in the city off and on all morning and in the afternoon up until an hour earlier. At 3:40 P.M., the clouds to the north are lifting; but to the southwest the sky is still dark, and what can be seen of the sun behind the overcast looks like a low-watt electric bulb shining through thick gray drapes. The temperature which the rain has cooled to the low 70s throughout the earlier part of the day is rising into the 80s, along with increasing humidity. But that's outside, and in the T-Bird the windows are up and the air conditioner is on.

To reach the 79th Street Marina from Riverside Drive, you have to follow a cloverleaf of multilevel roads that wind down and around the western tip of Riverside Park to the water's edge.

Julia Angstrom has been nervous all during the ride over from her apartment, and has said very little. She's wearing a white linen dress with blue piping around the collar, a blue linen jacket, and white sling-back pumps. She keeps crossing and uncrossing her legs restlessly, and the knuckles of her right hand are bloodless from the tight grip she has on the handle of the cowhide attaché case in her lap.

The road up ahead curves and dips into a circular underground drive which leads finally to a gloomy, cavernous garage under Riverside Park. There are maybe fifty or more cars parked there, and there's still plenty of room.

When the T-Bird rolls to a stop, Julia Angstrom says, with a tremor in her voice, "Wish us both good luck." She reaches a hand to open the car door. Before she can get out, the car phone buzzes. She looks startled.

"It's okay. Sit tight for a moment."

The phone buzzes again.

"Yeah, hello? This is J. T. Spanner."

"Spanner, Sergeant Hornstein. I called your office, and they told me to try you on your car phone."

"You got me, sergeant. What's up?"

"You remember that body we found we thought might be Jill Balfe's?" Hornstein asks. "Well, we just got the word from the morgue. It wasn't her. Forensic made a positive fingerprint I.D. on the corpse. Some dame who was reported missing three weeks ago after she came to New York on a visit from Oregon. Hell of a distance to come to wind up stuffed in a sewer. I thought you'd want to know it wasn't Jill Balfe."

"I did want to know. Thanks, sergeant."

"Anything new to report at your end?"

"I'm still running down leads, here and there."

"You let me know you find anything," Hornstein says.

"Yeah, right."

Hornstein hangs up.

"That was a police sergeant in Missing Persons, Mrs. Angstrom. They had a body they thought might be Jill Balfe's. Turns out it wasn't."

"I could have told them that," she says, getting out of the car.

There's a short tunnel leading out of the subterranean parking area to a wide concrete walk which runs parallel to the river. Just outside the mouth of the tunnel is the marina: a series of narrow wooden piers zigzagging out into the water with yachts, cruisers, sailboats, and a couple of houseboats docked alongside. The marina is enclosed by a low steel-mesh fence, and there are two steel-mesh gates, approximately a block apart, leading to the piers. The air from the water has a hot, tarry smell.

The nearest gate is just a few paces north of the mouth of the tunnel. The gate has a sign on it:

PRIVATE DOCK
BOAT OWNERS ONLY

Julia Angstrom ignores the sign, strides through the gate and, saying, "This way, Mr. Spanner," steps carefully onto one of the piers extending out into the river. She points to a large, square silver-and-black houseboat moored at the far end of the pier. "That's Duane's there."

There are people puttering around on the decks of various boats inside the marina. The river water on either side of the pier is dark and oily. It looks like across the river, the far bank, the Jersey side where there are a line of apartment buildings, is so near you could toss a silver dollar from shore to shore with ease.

Out on the end of the pier there's a short gangplank to the narrow deck which circles the outside of Vinton's houseboat. Julia Angstrom crosses to the deck first and raps on the cabin door, which is toward the bow. She knocks on the door several more times and when there's still no answer, she turns her head and says anxiously, "Do you suppose the whole thing was just another of his hoaxes?"

"Better let me try the door. Just in case. I'm armed." The gun in the clip-on holster is a .38 Police Special since Kauffman and Tynan are still holding the Magnum.

The door isn't locked. It opens and swings inward. The houseboat rocks gently on the swells of the river beneath.

"Stay out here till I take a look inside."

Just inside the door is a bloody handprint slapped against the wall. It's difficult to know what the interior of the houseboat looked like before, because now it's in a shambles. It's one long, open area running from bow to stern, and in it furniture is upturned all over the place. The upholstered chairs, cushions, mattresses have been gutted open, and the stuffing inside yanked out. The carpeting has been ripped up and slashed; pictures from the walls lie smashed on the floor; books, papers, and records are scattered from one end of the place to the other.

There's more blood splattered on the wall about midway down the inside of the houseboat, a large smear that's still wet and has strands of darkish blond hair sticking to it. Half a dozen paces farther on, there are two broken teeth lying on the carpet. There's a lopsided circle of blood, about two feet in diameter, in front of the door in the stern. The inside doorknob is sticky with blood. Outside the door, on the deck, there's a ragged trail of blood across the wooden planking and, on the railing, more blood. Over the side of the railing is a straight drop to the river. It's not hard to guess that somebody dragged a bloody body out of the houseboat and deep-sixed it in the Hudson.

There's a small, stifled scream from inside the houseboat. Back in there, Julia Angstrom is standing inside the doorway near the bow, gazing about her in shock. She looks up. Her eyes are glazed. She turns suddenly and rushes out the door.

"Mrs. Angstrom! Mrs. Angstrom!"

She doesn't pause, doesn't turn her head, just keeps running up the pier, the attaché case swinging at her side, and out through the gate.

It's either go after her, or take time to poke around inside the houseboat for clues before the police arrive.

After fifteen, twenty minutes of searching through the books and papers littering the floor there doesn't seem to be anything of significance except for two items: one, a copy of *The Encyclopedia of Precious Gems* compiled by Sir James Moncrief, with the corners of the pages turned down in the chapter on the Sancy Diamond; and, two, Duane Vinton's photograph album which is filled with pictures of him and an assortment of his female conquests in various stages of dress and undress and scenes of him and a companion—one or another—in what might be called erotic situations. The book and the album are going out of there before the cops arrive.

Now there's a sound at the door near the bow and it swings open. Benny Orkin steps through and literally freezes in mid-stride, only his head moving from side to side as his eyes take in the scene inside the houseboat. He starts to scramble back out the door.

"Just hold it, Benny! See this gun in my hand? You make one more move out that door and I'm going to put a bullet in you."

Orkin stops and then reluctantly steps back through the door.

"That's better. Come over here. You got a gun stuffed in the back of your pants?"

"N-no-no, Jesus, no," Orkin stammers. "I ain't packing." He lifts his jacket and shirt and turns completely around.

"All right. Now what are you doing here?"

"Listen," Orkin says, "what happened here? Juh-Juh-Jesus!"

"I don't know what happened. The place was like this when I got here. I asked you what you were doing here?"

"I was—it was—I just decided to come by and see if by chance Vinton had showed up here. You know, after the talk you and me had about how I'd try to turn him up for you."

"It's no good, Benny. You came here to meet Vinton—"

"Where'd you get that?" he asks. "I ain't—"

"Knock it off, goddammit. Vinton called you. He called you yesterday when I was there in the room with you. He told you the payoff was to be today and to meet him here."

"Payoff? What the fuck—"

"You're trying my patience, Benny. I *know* about the diamond. I know you were in on it with him. Bullshit me not."

Orkin's whole body sags. He starts sweating. "Listen," he says, "you got to give me time to get my head together. I got to think—"

"Suit yourself, Benny. I don't give a damn whether you talk to me or not. I'm turning you over to the cops."

"Listen, just give me some—"

"No more time, Benny. *Move.* Out the door. I'll be right behind you. The gun's in my coat pocket. You so much as think of trying any tricks, or running, and you're going to buy it."

Orkin moves out through the door and is very careful to keep only a step or two ahead on the way up the pier and in through the tunnel to the garage. There are a row of public telephones inside the tunnel, but there are people using two of the phones. It'll be better to call the police from the car phone.

Over at the T-Bird, the phone is buzzing.

"Get in, Benny."

Orkin crawls in the door, his eyes on the buzzing phone. The book and the photo album from Vinton's houseboat go on the seat beside him.

"Yeah, hello, this is Spanner."

"*J. T.? J. T.? Oh, thank God!*" Bobbie Gillian's voice at the other end of the line comes in a shaky whisper: "*There are two men here in the apartment. They've got Karen in the living room. They're wrecking the place.*

They don't know I'm here, in the bedroom. I called you first. Now I'm going to call the police—"

"I'll call the police, Bobbie. You stay hidden, if you can. I'm on my way there. Stay quiet."

"Jesus," Benny Orkin says. "What's going on?"

"Shut up, Benny."

The switchboard operator at the 16th Precinct picks up the call on the first ring.

"Let me have Captain Tynan quick. It's urgent."

Tynan comes on the line almost immediately and says, "Homicide. Capt—"

"This is J. T. Spanner, captain. Listen carefully. There's a hell of a big case unraveling fast. Right now somebody—two guys—are in that apartment where Jill Balfe lived. The two roommates are there. The guys are apparently holding one of the girls. The other one's hidden in the bedroom. She called me. She says the guys are wrecking the place. You know the address—600 East Thirty-eighth Street. It's Apartment 4J. Get some cars over there fast, huh? Tell them no sirens. I'm on my way there—"

"Got it," Tynan says. "I'm on my way, too."

"Okay. But listen, there's more. I'm just leaving Duane Vinton's houseboat at the Seventy-ninth Street Marina. I think somebody slaughtered somebody in there and then dropped the body off the stern of the houseboat into the river. Better get some men there, too, and some divers. Also, you want to pick up a Mrs. Julia Angstrom fast. She lives at 642 Park Avenue, Apartment 12K. She's involved. You can pick her up as a witness. I'll explain when I see you at the girls' apartment—"

"Spanner—"

"I'm going to have to hang, captain."

Benny Orkin slumps down dejectedly in the car seat.

"Look alert, Benny. Look alert. We're going to fly low. I don't know what we're going to find when we get there but I have a feeling we're nearing the finish line."

186

> TOW-AWAY ZONE
> NO PARKING
> AT ANY TIME
> DEPT. OF TRAFFIC
>
> ——*Sign in front of 600 East 38th Street*

BECAUSE there are private cars parked at the curb, at least half of them with DPL—Diplomatic—license plates which make them immune to the city's parking laws, three squad cars are double-parked in the street in front of 600 East 38th Street. Two more squad cars and an unmarked police car turn the corner at First Avenue, come down the street, and also double-park in front of the building. The uniformed patrolmen from the squad cars are standing near the entrance to the building, apparently waiting for orders. Inspector Max Kauffman, Captain John Tynan, and four plainclothesmen get out of the unmarked car.

Kauffman and Tynan come over to the T-Bird, which is also double-parked, behind the squad cars.

"I want to know what this is all about, Spanner," Tynan says.

"There's no time now. We've got to get upstairs fast."

"You better be goddamn positive of what you're

doing," Tynan says. Then he looks at Inspector Kauffman. The inspector nods his head.

Tynan jerks a thumb at Benny Orkin. "What about him?"

"He goes, too. He's part of it. But you may have to drag him."

Tynan gives Benny Orkin a hard look. "I don't want any trouble from you. Understand?"

Benny Orkin spreads his hands. "No trouble, man." He's shaking so hard that his teeth almost chatter. Tynan turns away, and Benny Orkin leans close and asks nervously, "What's that book you got there from Vinton's houseboat, Spanner?"

"It's an encyclopedia, Benny. I'm taking college courses by mail."

Inspector Kauffman waves a hand in the air. "Let's go up," he says curtly.

Tynan dispatches some of the officers around to cover the rear of the building and leaves a couple more men in the apartment house lobby. The rest of the group crowds into the elevator and rides up to the fourth floor.

When the elevator doors open, the police swiftly fan out around the door to Apartment 4J. The inspector and Tynan both draw their guns, one on either side of the doorway. The other police, guns drawn, are standing behind the two ranking officers.

Tynan makes a motion to one of the plainclothesmen, and the man moves up to the door. He takes a ring of keys out of his pocket. Carefully and silently, he tests the keys in the lock one after another until, on the fifth or sixth try, he nods his head. He turns the key in the lock, turns the doorknob, and crashes the door back on its hinges. The police pour into the room.

There are two men in the room, one kneeling in front of the sofa, slashing the sofa cushions with a switchblade, the other holding a revolver and standing beside Karen Rushler who's sitting in a chair, her arms crossed over her chest.

"All right! Drop the gun, drop the knife!" Inspector Kauffman orders, swinging the muzzle of his gun from one man to another. The man with the gun lets it fall to the carpet. The other man leaves the knife sticking in one of the sofa cushions and stands. Both men look to be about forty-some years old, and both of them are dressed in dark suits.

The man who was holding the gun looks around the room, almost insolently, at all the guns aimed at him. "What the hell is this, inspector?" he asks.

"*I'll* ask *you*, Crommer," Inspector Kauffman says to the man. "What the hell is this?"

The man the inspector has called "Crommer" jerks his head toward his companion who had had the knife. "Ludler and I been working on an investigation." He shrugs. "Maybe we haven't exactly been following the rule book, but why this show of force?"

Crommer is over six feet tall, heavy-set, has dark, bushy hair, and large facial features—his nose looks like it's been broken sometime in the past. Ludler is an inch shorter than six feet, weighs about 180, has lost most of his sandy hair, and has a kind of aging boyish face, the skin of which is very fair and spotted with freckles.

Inspector Kauffman looks puzzled. He turns his head and says, "Now I'm going to ask you, Spanner, what the hell is this?"

"Who are these men, inspector?"

The inspector points to one and then the other. "Sergeant Crommer, Sergeant Ludler. They're on the robbery detail. So I'm asking you again, Spanner, what the hell's this is all about?"

"I don't know yet, inspector. What were they looking for here?"

Inspector Kauffman still looks puzzled. "I don't

know." He turns to Crommer again. "What were you looking for in here?"

Crommer says, "Ludler and I got a tip that there was some stolen stuff stashed in this apartment. We were working on an investigation on our own, hoping we'd uncover something."

The inspector starts to say, "Spanner—"

"Wait a minute, inspector. Where did they get a tip like that?"

Crommer tries to say something, but Inspector Kauffman interrupts. "I think I can answer that, Spanner. For the past several months, Crommer and Ludler have been part of a police fake-fencing operation. They've been working out of a storefront on Ninth Avenue and Forty-seventh Street, collecting evidence on crooks who brought their loot in for fencing. We made a hundred arrests in the case. The story broke in the newspapers day before yesterday—"

"A fake fencing operation? Yeah, I remember I read about it, day before yesterday. Give me a minute to think, inspector . . . yeah, I think I've got it. I think it all holds together—"

"Goddammit, Spanner," Tynan says disgustedly, "it better hold together, whatever it is."

Bobbie Gillian has slipped into the room. She's standing over by the windows. She looks scared to death. Karen Rushler has relaxed in her chair and lighted a cigarette.

"Come on, Spanner, tell it!" Inspector Kauffman says impatiently.

"It may sound complicated, but I'll try to keep it simple. There's a woman named Mrs. Julia Angstrom. She deals in rare gems. Very profitable business. She lives on Park Avenue, has a firm in the Diamond District. Deals with very exclusive, very wealthy clients—"

"We've picked her up on your say-so," Tynan says. "She's at the precinct."

"Uh-huh, good, captain. Now, as she tells it, when she

comes across a really rare gem and then sells it to one of her clients, the entire transaction is done in total secrecy because her clients do not want it known when they purchase such a rarity, both because of the notoriety and because of possible thefts. Okay? So, according to her, just recently, she was offered one of the most valuable diamonds in the world. Tell me, inspector, have you ever heard of the Sancy Diamond?"

Inspector Kauffman shakes his head.

"Well, inspector, I have a book here which will tell you all about it."

The inspector takes the book by Sir James Moncrief and glances at the title.

"You can read it some time at your leisure, inspector. For right now, let me tell you that the Sancy has a history as long as your arm, and is worth—God only knows how much. That much is a fact. So, now, Julia Angstrom has a chance to buy and sell the Sancy. Only there's one catch."

"Yeah, go on, Spanner, go on," Inspector Kauffman says impatiently.

"The catch is the diamond's in Europe and Mrs. Angstrom and her client are here in the U.S. You remember that these transactions have to be carried out in secret—and that leaves the problem of customs. Apparently, it's a problem she's had before. Which brings us to Duane Vinton."

"Vinton?" Tynan asks. "The guy who used to work at the health spa downstairs and who disappeared?"

"The very same. Julia Angstrom used to be a member of the spa. She met Vinton there. He's a hustler. He told her he could solve the customs problem for her. Apparently, he did—at least for a while."

"How?" Inspector Kauffman asks.

"Mrs. Angstrom claims she has no knowledge of what he did or how he did it or when. But my guess brings us to the missing airline stewardess—"

"Jill Balfe?" Tynan asks.

"Yeah. Like I said, apparently Vinton, using Jill Balfe, managed to solve the customs problem for Mrs. Angstrom—up to the Sancy Diamond. She—Mrs. Angstrom—made a mistake there. She told Vinton all about the Sancy. Vinton never made good on the delivery. In fact, he, Jill Balfe, and the diamond all dropped out of sight. Mrs. Angstrom thinks Vinton planned it that way—either to find his own buyer for the diamond, or to drive up the price he was going to demand of her."

The inspector raises his eyebrows. "How exactly do you know all this stuff about this Angstrom woman?"

"She told me. She hired me last night to do a job for her today. She was the one who originally hired Harry Flescher to look for Vinton. She heard about me from Flescher before he was killed. Incidentally, his death—all that drug stuff with Gregory Janish at the spa—apparently had no connection with this case. The two things just happened to overlap because of the spa."

"What was this job she hired you for?" Tynan asks.

"Yesterday morning she received a phone call from Vinton. He told her to meet him at his houseboat over at the Seventy-Ninth Street Marina at four P.M. today and she could have the diamond in exchange for two hundred and fifty thousand dollars. She got the money. She wanted me to go with her in case it was a trick."

"So you went," Tynan says, "that right?"

"We went, yeah. But somebody had been there ahead of us. Somebody who must have been watching for Vinton to show up there, must have known about the diamond. The place was in a shambles—like it might have been here if we hadn't gotten here in time—and there was a lot of blood around. It's my opinion that somebody killed Vinton for the diamond, sank the body in the Hudson, wrecked his houseboat to find it, and then came here looking for it. And, incidentally, they'd been here before, when the girls were away, searching this apartment, ever since Vinton disappeared. They were looking for the diamond then, or for a connection between Vinton and one of the girls."

"You're talking about Crommer and Ludler," Inspector Kauffman says sharply.

"I guess I am, yeah."

The inspector bites his lip. "You got any proof Crommer and Ludler knew about the diamond?"

"Proof? I guess that brings us to Benny Orkin, standing right here."

"M-M-Mm-me?" Benny Orkin sputters. "No, man, no, no, not me."

"Yeah, you, Benny. You were involved with Vinton. When Vinton decided to double-cross Mrs. Angstrom and try to find a buyer of his own for the diamond, you'd be the one he'd come to. You've always known about things like that: where to unload hot goods. In fact, a big-time fencing operation like Crommer and Ludler here were involved in, you'd sure as hell have gotten the word on that. You set it up between them and Vinton—not knowing the operation was a fake."

Orkin is shaking his head violently, the sweat dripping off him.

"Ah, yes, Benny, that's the way it was. And the day the story broke that the operation was a fake, day before yesterday, was when you panicked and went into hiding. And that's when Vinton knew, too, and knew he had to deal with Julia Angstrom. You called me, Benny, because you needed dough. And you fed me just enough information about Vinton to keep me on the hook—but all the time, you were concealing the real truth from me. You were in, Benny."

"Where'd you get all this"—Orkin remembers the two women in the room and says—"B.S.? Look, I don't know nothing, I ain't saying nothing. And nobody can make me, you understand?"

"Nobody's going to *make* you say anything, Benny. But for your own good, maybe you ought to do a little thinking right here and now. You may never get another chance. If you did steer Vinton to those two guys there, then you *know* they killed Vinton. You let them walk out of here free, and they're going to kill you, Benny. Sooner or later. You don't talk now, they'll still always be afraid you're going to, one day. So they'll have to shut you up."

Orkin's got his eyes screwed shut; his whole body's shaking like he's having a seizure. There's not a sound in the room. Suddenly Orkin's head begins to nod. It keeps on nodding up and down, up and down, as if he can't control it, and the words come blurting out of his mouth: "It's the way you said, exactly the way you said."

Orkin pauses to wipe the sweat off his face with the back of his hand and says, speaking rapidly, as if he's afraid he won't keep talking if he doesn't get it all out now, "Duane came to me before the rock was due to get here. He wants a buyer for it. I tell him about this big fence place I heard of, and we go over there and talk to those two guys." Orkin still has his eyes shut, but he points in the general direction of Crommer and Ludler. "They're hot to make the buy. Then the night that stewardess brings it in at Kennedy, something fuc—something fouls up—I don't know what. Vinton never tells me. But he calls me. He's scared, I can tell. He's been holed up in some hotel in Times Square—for a week or so. He wouldn't tell me where, he's scared to, but he tells me he's got the rock. He tells me those two guys—neither him nor I knew they were cops at that particular time—were trying to cross him to get the piece of goods."

Orkin pauses and gulps down air. Then he says, "The day the story broke in the papers about the fence place was a fake run by cops, Duane calls me again and tells me to get out of sight. I go hide in a hotel, too. Yesterday Vinton calls me at the hotel. He's having the trots over all that stuff that's going on at the spa, that private detective getting snuffed, you, Spanner, icing Janish. You don't know it, but you're getting to him just by nosing around

In addition to which, he's edgy that the two cops running the fake fence game are going to get to him. He says today he's going to unload the rock to the dame he had the deal with originally. He says I come to his houseboat today, he'll get me my share and we'll both split."

"What about the girl, Benny—the stewardess, Jill Balfe?"

Orkin shrugs. "He never mentioned her. But you're right, you're right, Spanner. Them was the two guys, all right." He opens his eyes and points first at Ludler, and then Crommer.

"Sonofabitch!" Inspector Kauffman says explosively, glaring at Crommer and Ludler. Then he turns and says, "All right, Spanner, since you seem to have all the answers, what about the diamond, this Sancy? Was it the real thing? Where is it now?"

"Well, I'll tell you, inspector. Julia Angstrom has a theory that Vinton and Jill Balfe were in this thing together, that they heard a call on the police radio—that night that he disappeared—about a girl's body being found over in Queens and they, Vinton and Jill Balfe, stole this body to confuse the case. She—Julia Angstrom—has worked this theory out pretty carefully. If she's right, then it's possible Jill Balfe is somewhere with the diamond."

"I take it," the inspector says dryly, "that you don't necessarily agree with her theory?"

"I don't. No. If my hunch is correct, we'll probably never know if the stone was the real Sancy."

"Why's that?"

"That book I gave you a few minutes ago about the Sancy Diamond? That book came from Vinton's houseboat. Julia Angstrom has a copy, too. She told me some of the stuff that's in the book about the Sancy. There's one famous incident that occurred in the diamond's history. It happened when a courier was delivering the diamond to some king and was jumped by thieves and killed. But the courier swallowed the diamond before he died. My hunch is Vinton, knowing the story, could have done the same thing if he had no other out. And the diamond went into the river with his body."

A quick, murderous look passes between Crommer and Ludler. The inspector sees it. He doesn't say anything, but the back of his neck flushes brick-red.

"So, inspector, unless your divers are lucky and dredge up Vinton's body, I don't guess we'll ever know whether the stone was really the famous Sancy Diamond."

Inspector Kauffman expels his breath in a long sigh. Then he motions to Crommer and Ludler and Orkin and says to his men, "Take them in. Book them for questioning. Captain Tynan and I will be along shortly."

While the men are leaving, the inspector lights up a cigar. He takes a couple of puffs, and after all the other policemen, except Captain Tynan, have gone, herding Benny Orkin, Crommer and Ludler out of the apartment he says, "It's going to be a bitch of a case to prosecute. However"—he lowers his voice so Bobbie Gillian and Karen Rushler, on the other side of the room, can't hear—"I figure we'll give this Angstrom dame immunity, she'll talk. That'll help. And we'll make a deal with this Orkin character, for a reduced sentence and he'll testify. Then we try to find some witnesses at the marina who might have noticed Crommer and Ludler around there today and can identify them."

The inspector takes a couple of puffs on his cigar. "If your hunch about all this is correct, Spanner, what about the stewardess, Jill Balfe? Where is she?"

"I don't know. She could be dead; she could be hiding; it could be we'll never know what happened to her."

Inspector Kauffman takes another couple of puffs on his cigar. "Guys like Crommer and Ludler—if they're guilty—give the department a bad name. Everybody's going to be crying 'crooked cops.' But it happens—cops sometimes get tempted like everybody else."

He aims his cigar. "Tell me something, Spanner. Sup

pose you and the Angstrom woman had recovered the Sancy Diamond, and she offered you a fancy price to keep the whole thing quiet, what would you have done?"

"Why, hell, inspector, you ought to know the answer to that."

Inspector Kauffman grunts. He waves a hand at Bobbie Gillian and Karen Rushler, says, "Goodnight, ladies," and he and Tynan leave.

Bobbie Gillian comes over quickly and lifts her lips for a kiss. Then she says, "Thank you for getting here so quick, J. T. And thank God, it's all over, at last!" She smiles. "Take me somewhere and feed me, huh? And let's be quiet together."

"You just made yourself a deal, honey."

Karen Rushler is still sitting in the chair, smoking a cigarette.

"What are you going to do, Karen? You want to go to dinner with us? You got a date?" Bobbie asks.

Karen Rushler waves a hand in the air. "You two run along," she says with a smile. "I'm going to bed. I haven't had such an exhausting time and so much fun since the last time I got laid."

Bobbie laughs. "You're terrible, Karen."

> Five hundred new members of the New York City Police Department and their families will attend a meeting at the Police Academy tonight to be addressed by ranking police officials before the new recruits receive assignment . . .
>
> ——*News 88, CBS Radio*

FROM the road up in Riverside Park there's a clear view through the T-Bird's windshield of the 79th Street Marina down below. The wide concrete walkway just outside the steel-mesh fence of the marina is now lined with police cars, police emergency vans, and two flatbed trucks with giant searchlights mounted on them. The powerful beams of the searchlights play across the piers, the boats, the river water inside the fence of the marina, lighting up the darkness for the police who are moving back and forth across the piers. The sweep of the searchlights extends to the waters out beyond the stern of Duane Vinton's silver-and-black houseboat. The deck of the stern of the houseboat is crowded with policemen—Inspector Kauffman and Captain Tynan probably among them—who have lowered grappling hooks over the railing in an attempt to fish for Vinton's body. A few yards farther out in the river, a dozen police launches and a couple of barges ride at anchor or circle slowly around the area of water where the police divers have gone down. Across the river, the Jersey Palisades glitter with lights from the windows of the apartment buildings lining the shores of the Hudson. Heat lightning flickers in the dark night sky to the west behind the Palisades.

Dozens of spectators—some of them families with children—are also lined up along the upper road in Riverside Park, watching the free show the police are putting on in the Hudson River below.

"Are we going to stay here much longer, J. T.?" Bobbie Gillian asks, her head leaning back against the car seat. She's smoking a cigarette.

"I was just curious, honey, to see what kind of a job the police were doing here. But we can leave if you like."

"I'd like," she says. "This spooks me. I thought the whole nightmare was finally over. You don't think they're going to find his body, do you?"

"Nope. Not in a million years. The current's probably swept it out to sea by now."

"Then, let's go, can we?"

"Sure. One thing before we leave. Reach between the seats, will you? There's a photograph album there I want you to take a look at. I'll turn on the dome light."

The puzzled expression on her face shows in the light from the car dome as she leans over and reaches a hand between the two seats. She lifts up the photograph album from Duane Vinton's houseboat and puts it in her lap.

"What's this?"

"Open it."

She opens the cover of the album and flips through a couple of pages.

"I found the album in Duane Vinton's houseboat today."

She only glances at a couple of pages and then closes the album wordlessly.

"He took good pictures, Bobbie."

"He was a camera nut." Her voice is dull and lifeless.

"You make a good model, too."

She turns sideways in the seat. "Don't you see, J. T., I hadn't met you then—"

"Nice try, honey. But that's not what we're talking about. Who am *I* to sit in judgment on another person's sex life? What we're talking about is it's obvious, from the photographs in the album, that you were Duane Vinton's girlfriend—the star of the album, certainly his closest girl friend—not Jill Balfe. There are no pictures of her in there. Not even with her clothes on."

Bobbie makes no answer.

"Bobbie, look, you know you've got to tell me about it. You know where Jill Balfe is. You know the whole story. You have to tell me. There's no other way."

She's silent for a moment. Finally, she nods her head slowly. There are tears in her eyes. Then she says, "Yes. I know I have to tell you. I think I've known that ever since I first met you. The whole time since then, I've felt like a pull-toy, my emotions tugged this way and that. Now I want to tell you." A couple of tears roll down her cheeks. "Let's take that ride now, can we?"

"Yeah. Where are we headed?"

"To Staten Island. Across the Verrazano Bridge."

The shortest route from Riverside Park is under the West Side Highway down to the tip of Manhattan. Bobbie sits slumped down in the seat, staring straight ahead. Traffic is light. Out in the Hudson River, alongside the Drive, there are a few tankers drifting southward in the darkness. Heat lightning still skip-flashes across the sky to the west.

"You okay, Bobbie?"

"I'm . . . a . . . fool," she says in a choked voice.

"You want to talk about it?"

"When we get there. Please, J. T."

She doesn't say anything else on the long drive through the Brooklyn Battery Tunnel, across Brooklyn, and to the Verrazano Bridge.

At the far end of the bridge, on Staten Island, Bobbie rouses herself.

"Stay on the expressway," she says. "We have a distance to go yet. I'll tell you when to slow down for the turnoff."

The expressway rolls on for miles through Staten Island before she says, "See that intersection coming up just ahead? Bear left."

The road leads down and around, and she says, "At the next street, turn right."

The street leads through a residential area, but soon the houses are farther and farther apart. A quarter of a mile beyond the last house, Bobbie says, "Turn left. Stay on this road down to the end."

Another quarter of a mile . . . a half mile . . . a mile . . . there are no houses around now, no lights anywhere, and soon, up ahead, the pavement comes to an end. As the T-Bird slows to a stop, the headlights sweep across what look like white hills rising up out of an open, marshy basin of land with a body of water in the distance. Here and there the flames of small fires are weaving sinuously in the dark air. There's a foul smell in the air, even with the car windows closed and the air conditioner on. At second glance, the white hills turn out to be huge mounds of garbage and refuse rising fifty to sixty feet in the air. Some of the mounds are burning. Several monstrous earth-moving machines stand atop the towering garbage heaps. Now the reek from the festering dump is almost overpowering.

Bobbie points to the mountains of trash. "Most of the garbage from Manhattan is towed out here by the Sanitation Department." In a shaky voice, she adds, "Jill Balfe is somewhere under there."

Jesus.

Bobbie weeps soundlessly for several minutes.

"It's all right, honey. The worst is over. Take your time. You can tell me about it when you're ready."

She uses a handkerchief from her handbag to wipe her

eyes, clears her throat several times, and lights a cigarette with trembling hands.

"I think I can do it now," she says. "Duane buried Jill's body there the night she disappeared. I was with him."

"He didn't kill Jill, did he?"

She shakes her head. "Back there in the apartment when you told the police what you thought had happened and what that Julia Angstrom thought had happened, you almost had the whole story just the way it did happen—except for a few minor differences."

She pauses and dabs at her eyes. "For almost a year, Duane had used Jill to smuggle gems into the country for Julia Angstrom. Jill had a schoolgirl crush on Duane and was eager to please him, and he took advantage of that to use her. She thought it was a big lark. There were no problems up to that last time. I knew all this because, you see, you were right. I was Duane's girlfriend, and he told me everything. But I was never involved until this last time."

Bobbie pauses again. "This last time," she says, "i was like you said about Duane knowing what the diamond was—the Sancy. She—Julia Angstrom—told him about it He'd even gotten that book and read up on the history o it. Well, he decided it was a chance to make a fortune fo himself. Double-cross her." She nods her head. "He used Benny Orkin to try to find a buyer for it. They talked to those two men—"

"Crommer and Ludler, that who you mean?"

"Yes. Duane and Benny didn't know the men wer cops, of course. Duane thought they were big-time fences He thought he had a deal all set with them. Boy, was h ever wrong."

"What happened?"

"When Jill landed at JFK that night, after the trip fro Antwerp, she was supposed to meet Duane and me at th airport and turn the diamond over to Duane, and the thre of us were going to drive back into the city. Well, Duar was there and I was there, but Jill never showed up. That is, she went through customs, all right, but she vanished between there and the U.S.-G. Airlines Building, where I was waiting for her. Duane was waiting outside, for both of us."

Bobbie takes a deep breath before she continues. "It took me a while to realize something had happened to her. I went outside. Duane was there. All the time he had thought she was inside the building. He had me check customs, and I found out she'd been through there. Duane was frantic. He guessed right away what must have gone wrong."

"Yeah? What was that?"

Bobbie sighs. "That the two men he'd been dealing with must have followed him in the days before Jill made the flight. Duane saw a lot of her during those days, and the men must have connected her up with him and figured out that she'd be bringing the diamond in. That night, when she didn't meet us, Duane said right away that they must have grabbed her and taken her somewhere so they could get the diamond away from her."

Bobbie stops talking, stubs out her cigarette, and lights another one. "Duane was like a wild man. He pulled me along to the car with him—not that I wouldn't have gone anyway—and we just kept driving around and around Queens, hoping we'd spot them. Incidentally, the reason Duane borrowed Julia Angstrom's car was because he *was* afraid somebody might know his own car and try to follow him from the airport with Jill and maybe make an attempt to get the diamond. He was always paranoid about things like that. But he never thought of the other thing happening."

"Why did you keep looking for them in Queens?"

"Duane had this idea," she says, "that whoever had Jill would try anything to get the diamond from her—even kill her—whether they got it or not. As it turned out, the idea wasn't that far out. You see, all the time we were driving,

Duane had the car radio tuned in to the police calls. When we heard the call come over the air that a woman's body had been found on the bridge, Duane said he knew it had to be Jill. And that we had to get the body. When we got to where it was and saw them put it in the morgue wagon, he decided we had to stop the morgue wagon and take the body. He had a gun. We put on the coveralls we found in the car and tore up my pantyhose to use as masks."

"But what was the point of stealing her body then?"

"Duane knew—and I knew, too, for that matter—that Jill would never tell where the diamond was. So she'd still have it."

"I don't under—"

"The diamond," Bobbie says softly, "it was in her— body. That's the way she always managed to smuggle them in past customs. The diamond would be embedded in a small wad of cotton packing which she would insert as far up as it would go inside her. It couldn't be detected except by an internal examination. In that case, she had learned how, through constant exercising, to develop her sphincter muscles and the muscles—I think they're called the levator and constrictor muscles—of her vagina so they would contract for long enough to conceal the diamond. Anyway, she never got caught."

"Well, yeah—"

"We recovered the diamond from her body." Bobbie stubs out her cigarette. "Duane knew about this dump. He'd once lived here on Staten Island. We drove over. He put her body in there."

Bobbie's voice is very tired. "There's not much more to tell. Between the stories in the newspaper about the body being stolen and Jill missing and Duane's fear of the two men coming after him, he decided he had to sell the diamond to Julia Angstrom."

"Then he did have it today?"

"Yes," she says. "And I think you're right about what

204

happened to it. That when those two men, who must have been watching the houseboat all along, saw Duane there and broke in, he swallowed it. It's the kind of thing he'd do. End of story."

She glances out the window. "Like I said, J. T., I'm a fool."

"Bobbie—"

"I know what you're going to say, J. T. That you have to call the police. Go ahead. The sooner this is all finished, the better."

The operator at the 16th Precinct has to relay the message on to Inspector Kauffman and Captain Tynan, who are still up at the 79th Street Marina. Fifteen minutes go by before the car phone buzzes and Inspector Kauffman says, "What's this all about, Spanner?"

"I think I've located Jill Balfe's body, inspector. And I've uncovered a few more facts to add to the case. I think you'd better come out here. Staten Island."

"Out where on Staten Island?"

"Hold on, inspector . . . Bobbie, where are we exactly?"

"This place is called Fresh Kills, and it's Sanitation Plants One and Two," Bobbie says.

"Okay, Spanner, I heard her," Inspector Kauffman says at the other end of the line.

"And inspector—bring those two creeps you're holding, Ludler and Crommer. Oh, you'd better bring somebody from the Sanitation Department, too, a commissioner or somebody. You'll see why when you get here."

"Yeah," Inspector Kauffman says and hangs up.

After a moment, Bobbie sits forward. "J. T.?"

"Yeah?"

"I'm scared. You know? What'll they do to me?"

"I don't know for sure, Bobbie. But I think they'll probably give you a break. You'll be cooperating with them. And I'll help you get a good lawyer."

Bobbie nods her head. She lights another cigarette. After a moment, she asks, "J. T., can we get another station on the radio, please? No more news. Some music."

"Sure, honey, you pick it."

She twists the dial until she finds some music. Then she sits back, smoking her cigarette. After a while she says, "J. T., in the beginning, I admit I was playing a game with you. All I wanted was to make sure you weren't getting too close to what happened. But not after the night we made love. Everything I felt about you after that was real."

Bobbie doesn't say anything else. There's nothing more to say.

> ... The garbage dump in Fresh Kills, Staten Island, opened in March 1974. During the first four months it was in operation 700 barges transported 500,000 tons of refuse from the City of New York and dumped it at the site. In the time since then it has become the world's biggest garbage dump ...

THERE are six cars of them when they finally arrive, sirens blaring, red lights flashing. Inspector Kauffman, Tynan, another man, a dozen uniformed patrolmen, and the two prisoners, Ludler and Crommer, in handcuffs, get out of the squad cars. The inspector and Tynan come over. Bobbie opens the car door.

Inspector Kauffman leans into the car. "All right, we're here, Spanner. What's this all about?"

"I'll tell you, inspector," Bobbie says. "I'll tell you all about it." She swings her legs around and gets out of the car. The inspector moves aside.

"Oh, inspector?"

"Yeah, Spanner?" He leans back into the car.

"I want to ask another favor."

"Yeah, what's that?"

"While she tells you what's what here, I want to have a word alone with your prisoner, Crommer. Okay?"

Max Kauffman frowns. "I don't know," he says doubtfully.

"Come on, inspector, come on! You can leave the cuffs on him. You still owe me."

"Yeah, well, all right."

Tynan stays with Bobbie while Inspector Kauffman crosses to where one of the patrolmen is guarding Crommer. Max Kauffman flips a thumb over his shoulder and says to the patrolman, "Spanner here wants to talk to Crommer privately. It's okay."

"Hey! What is this?" Crommer asks.

"Let's go, Crommer. Take a walk with me. Over this way."

Crommer doesn't like the idea much, but he shuffles on ahead across the uneven ground. After he's walked a couple of yards, he turns his head and says, "Where you taking me?"

"Keep walking."

Crommer drags his feet on for several more yards. The squad cars and the figures milling around them are now in the distance, out of hearing range. Just ahead, one of the dump piles is burning steadily, the blaze lighting up the night.

"Okay, Crommer, you can stop here."

Crommer turns and stands, the flames from the fire behind him illuminating his figure like a pool of spotlight.

"What do you want with me?" His voice is surly.

"I want to talk to you about the way you killed that girl."

"Fuck you."

"You're going to tell me about it, Crommer, if you want to live. How you killed her. Did it give you a kick? Torturing her with burning cigarettes, knocking her teeth down her throat, beating her to death? You're a tough man, huh, Crommer? Oh, yes, you're going to tell me all about it."

Crommer makes an obscene gesture with the middle finger of his manacled right hand. "I'm telling you nothing. Nobody's got nothing on me."

"Wrong, Crommer. You're carrying the proof of your guilt around with you. There's blood on your hands."

Crommer starts to make the obscene gesture with his finger again. The bullet from the .38 catches him dead center in the palm of his right hand. Blood spurts from the dark hole in the flesh. He screams, bends double, curses, blood dripping from the hand, both hands writhing in the steel cuffs. The second bullet hits him in the back of the left hand. He screams again and falls to his knees, clutching his bloody hands to his chest.

"I told you you had blood on your hands, Crommer."

On his knees, head hanging down, Crommer starts to curse again and then breaks off, gagging and half-retching, choking from the pressure of the tip of the barrel of the .38 jammed into the underside of his throat, against his windpipe.

"Listen to me, Crommer, you sonofabitch. It wouldn't take much for me to kill you right now. I'd like to. To repay you for what you did to that girl. I'd get away with it. I'd tell the cops you tried to jump me, and I shot you in both hands and then through the head. Now your only chance to live is to tell me where that car is that you killed the girl in. It's got to be soaked with her blood. You have five seconds to start talking. One—two—"

"Uh—uh—Ludler's car," he gasps hoarsely. "Hid it—garage—his summer—place—Pocono Mountains—Stroudsburg—Pennsylvania—it's there—"

Crommer's just gotten the last words out when Inspector Kauffman, Tynan, and several patrolmen come running up.

"What the hell's going on?" the inspector asks. They all have their guns drawn.

"It's all right, inspector. Everything's under control. He

tried to jump me and get away. I had to shoot him when he grabbed for my gun, but only in the hands."

"He's lying! He's lying!" Crommer yells hoarsely. "He shot me deliberately, tried to get me to confess—"

"Hold it, inspector. Hold it. He's the one who's lying. He caught me off guard. Tried to get the gun away. I had no choice."

"We'll talk about it," Max Kauffman says brusquely. He turns to his men, pointing to Crommer. "Get him out of here. Get him to a doctor." The inspector turns back. "Come on, Spanner, I want to talk to you."

Inspector Kauffman walks back toward where the squad cars are parked. For a moment, he's silent. Then he says, "Look, Spanner, goddammit—"

"Don't say anything else, inspector. Let me talk for a minute. Back there a moment ago, Crommer confessed where the car is that he and Ludler killed Jill Balfe in. They stashed it in the garage at Ludler's summer place in Stroudsburg, Pennsylvania, in the Pocono Mountains. That car's got to be soaked with her blood. You can match the types. You ought to be able to take it from there."

Max Kauffman swings around, hands on his hips. His voice is hard as he says, "Sure, and you're going to try to make me believe Crommer just happened to volunteer that information to you. For Christ's sake, he'll get some hotshot lawyer and yell that you shot him and threatened him to pry that information out of him and the court's squash the evidence."

"I'm not trying to make *you* believe anything, inspector. When the case goes into court, I'll gladly, willingly, testify that Crommer told me all that to throw me off guard and then made a grab for the gun."

Inspector Kauffman starts to say something else.

"No, wait, inspector. I have something else to say. Something we've got to get straight. Don't hassle me on this. I'm not one of your flunkeys anymore. Tonight was between Crommer and me. You're lucky I didn't kill him. I take individual responsibility for tonight and for whatever comes. You just make your case on the evidence you've got now. I'll see to it that it sticks."

"I still don't like it," Max Kauffman says, his voice sour. He shakes his head a couple of times and turns and stomps away to where Bobbie, Tynan, and some of the uniformed patrolmen are waiting. A couple of other patrolmen have loaded Crommer into a squad car, and the car drives away fast, up the dark road.

Back inside the T-Bird, in the air-conditioned coolness, the others—Bobbie, Inspector Kauffman, Tynan, the remaining patrolmen, as seen through the windshield—look like pantomime actors in some avant-garde play, lips moving, hands gesturing, pacing back and forth against the surrealistic landscape, the ghostly piles of garbage jutting up behind them like stage scenery, the sky intermittently lit by flashes of heat lightning.

Jill Balfe . . . the little girl in the photographs on the mantel in the house in the Bronx . . . in the confirmation dress . . . the bathing suit, with baby fat showing . . . on horseback . . . and now here . . . Jill and Bobbie . . . not evil, careless . . . still children, really, in women's bodies, vulnerable . . . playing games . . . making missteps blindly, innocently . . . unaware of the sometime savage brutality of reality . . . Jill and Bobbie and—and Ellie and Lee . . . where are *they* now, at this moment . . . are they safe . . . what are they doing?

The phone at Ellie's end of the line rings and rings and rings before she finally answers it breathlessly.

"Ellie? This is J. T. I was thinking about you, honey."

"Oh, hi, J. T. I was in the shower. Do you want to come over?"

"I'd like to, honey. I'd really like to. But I'm calling you from the car. I'm still out on the case. Tell you all about it tomorrow."

"Okay," she says. "I'm glad you called."

"I'll see you in the office in the morning. Goodnight, baby,"

"'Night, J. T."

When Lee answers her phone, she says: "Huh? Hello?"

"Lee, this is J. T."

"J. T.? What are you doing calling at this hour? I was asleep. You sound funny, J. T. Are you out somewhere drinking?"

"No. It's all right, darling, go back to sleep."

It's a long time before Inspector Kauffman and Bobbie come back to the car and open the door.

"I wanted to say goodnight, J. T.," Bobbie says. "And thanks." She lifts a hand and lets it drop.

"I'll come see you tomorrow, Bobbie, and we'll talk."

She nods and turns away.

Inspector Kauffman leans into the car. "I think this wraps it up, Spanner. The Sanitation Commissioner and I have to iron out the details on how to recover the body. Vinton's body, I don't think we'll ever find in the river now. But as far as the case goes, that's that." He starts to leave and then leans back into the car again. "Oh, and the department appreciates your help."

"Yeah."

They all leave, the car taillights disappearing up the road. There's darkness all around again except for the forks of heat lightning overhead and the few scattered dump fires burning slowly out into ashes.

Inspector Kauffman's already said it. Now nobody will ever know for sure whether the stone was really the Sancy Diamond or not. Vinton's body is in the river, Jill Balfe's body's under the mountains of garbage.

Soon they'll just be statistics, two out of the 90,000 some deaths which will be recorded in the city this year.

What else is there to say about it all? Maybe . . . maybe just that if lives can't be saved, deaths can be solved. There's that.

Lightning suddenly crackles close by in the darkness

thunder rolls through the night, and rain pours down, drenching the fires, streaming down the windows and windshield of the T-Bird.

The phone buzzes.

"Hello, J. T.? J. T., are you there?"

"I'm here, Lee."

"After you called, I couldn't get back to sleep. Your voice sounded so strange. When I thought about it, I realized you hadn't been drinking. Are you all right?"

There's something else, too, come to think of it. Now the faceless lady has amber eyes, a pretty face, jet-black hair cut short and curled under at the ends. She's dressed in a stylishly cut, gunmetal-gray stewardess's uniform with her cap set at a jaunty angle. Forever.

"I'm okay, Lee honey. I'm coming home."

It's a bright, sunny morning. The forecast is for a clear, hot day. The front-page news story is:

BODY OF MISSING GIRL BURIED UNDER 600 TONS OF GARBAGE

POLICE ANNOUNCED EARLY THIS MORNING THAT THE BODY OF AIRLINE STEWARDESS JILL BALFE, 26—WHO HAS BEEN MISSING—IS BURIED UNDER A 60-FOOT-DEEP MOUND OF GARBAGE, ACCORDING TO A WITNESS IN THE CASE. AUTHORITIES STATE THEY WILL NOT SEARCH THE NEARLY 30 ACRES OF REFUSE IN FRESH KILLS, STATEN ISLAND, TO RECOVER THE BODY SINCE THE JOB WOULD COST AN ESTIMATED $4 MILLION.

POLICE SAID THE VICTIM'S MOTHER, MRS. MARGARET BALFE, HAD AGREED THAT THE EXPENSE WAS TOO GREAT

TO TRY TO RECOVER THE BODY AND THAT SHE WAS SATISFIED AS TO HER DAUGHTER'S FATE.

ONE OF TWO MANHATTAN DETECTIVES ARRESTED IN THE CASE, SERGEANT KARL LUDLER, 44, HAS CONFESSED TO THE MURDER OF THE GIRL AND TO A SECOND SLAYING CONNECTED TO THE CASE, AND HAS IMPLICATED HIS PARTNER, DETECTIVE SERGEANT RALPH CROMMER, 48.

THE SECOND MURDER ALSO INVOLVES A MISSING BODY, THAT OF DUANE VINTON, 32, WHO IS ALLEGED TO HAVE BEEN KILLED AND THE BODY TOSSED INTO THE HUDSON RIVER. POLICE HAVE GIVEN UP THE SEARCH FOR HIS BODY BUT SAY THAT THEY ARE CONFIDENT THAT, BASED UPON OTHER EVIDENCE, THEY CAN CONVICT LUDLER AND CROMMER IN THE TWO HOMICIDES . . .

The New York Times

CHARTER BOOKS—The best in mystery and suspense!
JOHN CREASEY

"Consistently the most satisfying of mystery novelists."
—The New York Post

☐ **A SPLINTER OF GLASS**   77800-3 $1.50
A tiny clue was all Superintendent West had to solve a huge gold theft—and a murder.

☐ **THEFT OF MAGNA CARTA**   80554-X $1.50
Scotland Yard searches for international thieves before a priceless treasure vanishes.

CHARTER BOOKS—The best in guides for healthier living!

☐ **INSTANT HEALTH THE NATURE WAY**   37079-9 $1.50
Put natural foods to work to fortify your body against disease.   Carlson Wade

☐ **HERBAL REMEDIES**   32761-3 $1.95
The classic book of herbal medications, with centuries-old, proven remedies you can make.   Simmonite/Culpeper

☐ **INFANT CARE**   37058-6 $1.95
by U.S. Dept. of Health, Education and Welfare.
The most famous book in America on pregnancy and child care, revised and updated.

CHARTER BOOKS, Book Mailing Service
P.O. Box 690, Rockville Centre, N.Y. 11570

Please send me the titles checked above.

I enclose $ _____ . Add 50¢ handling fee per book.

Name _____

Address _____

City _____ State _____ Zip _____

Cb

NICK CARTER

"Nick Carter out-Bonds James Bond."
—<u>Buffalo Evening News</u>

Exciting, international espionage adventure with Nick Carter, Killmaster N3 of AXE, the super-secret agency!

☐ THE ULTIMATE CODE   84308-5 $1.50
Nick Carter delivers a decoding machine to Athens—and finds himself in a CIA trap.

☐ BEIRUT INCIDENT   05378-5 $1.50
Killmaster infiltrates the Mafia to stop a new breed of underworld killer.

☐ THE NIGHT OF THE AVENGER   57496-3 $1.50
From Calcutta, to Peking, to Moscow, to Washington, AXE must prevent total war.

☐ THE SIGN OF THE COBRA   76346-4 $1.50
A bizarre religious cult plus a terrifying discovery join forces against N3.

☐ THE GREEN WOLF CONNECTION   30328-5 $1.50
Middle-eastern oil is the name of the game, and the sheiks were masters of terror.

Available wherever paperbacks are sold or use this coupon.

CHARTER BOOKS, Book Mailing Service
P.O. Box 690, Rockville Centre, N.Y. 11570

Please send me the titles checked above.

I enclose $_____ . Add 50¢ handling fee per book.

Name_____

Address_____

City_____ State _____ Zip_____

Db

NICK CARTER

"America's #1 espionage agent."
—Variety

Don't miss a single high-tension novel in the Nick Carter Killmaster series!

☐ THE JERUSALEM FILE   38951-5 $1.50
Nick battles Arab terrorists who have kidnapped the world's ten wealthiest men.

☐ THE FILTHY FIVE   23765-7 $1.50
Killmaster uncovers a Chinese plot to assassinate the President of the United States.

☐ SIX BLOODY SUMMER DAYS   76838-5 $1.50
The search for a stolen nuclear missile sends AXE into a desert death trap.

☐ THE KATMANDU CONTRACT   43200-X $1.50
The fate of Asia depended on a billion dollars in diamonds at the roof of the world.

☐ THE Z DOCUMENT   95485-5 $1.50
A power-hungry general in the Ethiopian Sahara stops at nothing to dominate the globe.

Available wherever paperbacks are sold or use this coupon.

CHARTER BOOKS, Book Mailing Service
P.O. Box 690, Rockville Centre, N.Y. 11570

Please send me the titles checked above.

I enclose $_____. Add 50¢ handling fee per book.

Name_____

Address_____

City_____ State _____ Zip_____

Eb

CHARTER BOOKS
—the best in mystery and suspense!

JOHN DICKSON CARR
"...one of the all-time masters."
—Chicago Daily News

☐ BELOW SUSPICION 05394-7 $1.50
Dr. Gideon Fell plunges into a terrifying case of mass murder—and the devil.

☐ FIRE, BURN! 22910-7 $1.50
Inspector Cheviot hails a taxi on a foggy London night, and climbs out in 1829!

☐ THE PROBLEM OF THE GREEN CAPSULE 68052-6 $1.50
Master Detective Gideon Fell meets a fascinating man with a very dangerous hobby: poison.

Available wherever paperbacks are sold or use this coupon.

CHARTER BOOKS, Book Mailing Service
P.O. Box 690, Rockville Centre, N.Y. 11570

Please send me the titles checked above.

I enclose $_____$. Add 50¢ handling fee per book.

Name_____

Address _____

City_____ State _____ Zip_____

Fb

CHARTER BOOKS
—the best in mystery and suspense!

VICTOR CANNING
"One of the world's six best thriller writers."
— Reader's Digest

☐ **THE MASK OF MEMORY** 52055-3 $1.75
A chilling tale of espionage and counterespionage in a world without rules.

☐ **A FOREST OF EYES** 22949-2 $1.75
A British scientist working behind the iron curtain is dragged into a violent nightmare.

☐ **FIRECREST** 22916-6 $1.75
A dead scientist, his depraved mistress, a revenge-filled agent—and a terrifying secret.

Available wherever paperbacks are sold or use this coupon.

CHARTER BOOKS, Book Mailing Service
P.O. Box 690, Rockville Centre, N.Y. 11570

Please send me the titles checked above.

I enclose $_____ . Add 50¢ handling fee per book.

Name_____

Address_____

City_____ State _____ Zip_____

Gb

HEALTH AND BEAUTY—ADVICE FROM THE EXPERTS

☐ **IT'S IN TO BE THIN** 37489-1 $1.95
Lose weight eating hundreds of delicious recipes that are amazingly low in calories. Lois Lyons Lindauer

☐ **HONEY FOR HEALTH** 34267-1 $1.50
Not only is honey a delicious energy source, it's a beauty aid and medicine, too. Cecil Tonsley

☐ **HEALTH THE EASY WAY** 31968-8 $1.95
A complete guide to healthful living from one of the world's leading nutritionists. Lelord Kordel

☐ **DR. CARLTON FREDERICKS' LOW CARBOHYDRATE DIET** 49772-1 $1.95
Don't count calories, eat six meals a day, and still lose up to 15 pounds a week!

☐ **VITAMIN C: THE PROTECTIVE VITAMIN** 86539-9 $1.50
Recent findings about the natural, inexpensive vitamin that can prevent and cure disease. James Webster

☐ **THE 14-DAY MIRACLE MAKE-OVER PROGRAM** 24906-X $1.95
A head-to-toe program for women that promises beautiful results in only two weeks. Zina Provendie

Available wherever paperbacks are sold or use this coupon.

CHARTER BOOKS, Book Mailing Service
P.O. Box 690, Rockville Centre, N.Y. 11570

Please send me the titles checked above.

I enclose $ _____ . Add 50¢ handling fee per book.

Name _____

Address _____

City _____ State _____ Zip _____

Bb